Yuletide in Ireland & WALES

Yuletide in Ireland & WALES

19th-Century Christmas
Romances in Two
Delightful Stories

GINNY AIKEN
TAMELA HANCOCK MURRAY

BARBOUR
PUBLISHING

Lost and Found

by Ginny Aiken

And when he cometh home,
he calleth together his friends and neighbours,
saying unto them, Rejoice with me;
for I have found my sheep which was lost.

Prologue

Wales, October 1870

"I f I might be so presumptuous, sir," said Joseph, Mervyn Gwynne's sometime secretary, "begging pardon, of course, it is sheer folly to permit a daughter to evade her duty."

Mervyn sighed. Why did Joseph pick the worst moments to discuss ticklish matters? This latest episode of gout was his most debilitating yet, and he had no interest in mental calisthenics.

"I've told you more times than I can be bothered to count," he replied, "that Rhiannon is not evading her duty. She is in Cardiff to help my dear sister with those three hooligans Deirdre is raising."

"Humph!"

The snort didn't bode well for Mervyn's current misery. Joseph was nothing if not tenacious.

"The girl belongs at your side, sir. I'm certain Miss Deirdre—er—Mrs. Wylie can avail herself of the aid of any disadvantaged young woman from Cardiff. I'm certain many of those can be found there. Of course, Mrs. Wylie could always tame the little beasts herself."

"She's in the family way again, Joseph. And my sister has always been delicate. She needs help, and Rhiannon loves the little ones—who are not beasts, as you well know. They're merely healthy youngsters, who, by the way, dearly love Rhiannon, as well."

"Everyone loves Rhiannon, if I might say so myself." Joseph's squared jaw resembled a rock cliff. "But Cardiff, sir! The girl has likely lost every sense of who she truly is and from where she comes. I fear life in the big city has led her to put on all kinds of airs and affectations."

Mervyn tried to ease his left side but winced at the jab of pain. He shook his head. "She was still the sweet, spirited young woman I've always known the last time I visited."

"But that was nearly a year ago now. You couldn't join the family this past Easter, could you?"

"You're right. We had trouble at the mine at that time, and I could not leave. The last time I saw Rhiannon was, indeed, last Christmas."

"And we're now in the month of October. Our Lord's birth is almost upon us again. The girl should be here with you."

"Enough, Joseph!" Mervyn slid down his pillows to lie flat on the bed. "I'm in misery and don't wish to discuss this any further. I see no reason to drag my daughter back here where the mine and the accidents that happen too often filled her with fear all those years ago."

"She must face reality. She's no longer a child, and life is fraught with dangers—"

"I said enough, man. I intend to spend Christmas in Cardiff with her, as usual."

Joseph humphed again. "Should this curse of gout allow you."

"If the good Lord sees fit for me to travel."

Mercifully, Joseph didn't counter Mervyn's sentiment. The stubborn man left the room, and Mervyn turned to prayer. After a good long while of communion with his heavenly Father, he slept again.

A fortnight after Joseph's harangue on Rhiannon's supposed duties, Mervyn, in a mite less pain, thought the matter put to rest. He'd been making progress with his recovery, the mine had been running smoothly, and all seemed as normal as his life ever became. But he'd conveniently forgotten Joseph's unpredictability.

After the man regaled Mervyn with the latest details of that day's affairs at the mine, had him sign those documents that required his signature, and listened to Mervyn's directions regarding other matters of importance, he paused in the doorway to the room.

"Yes, Joseph?" Mervyn inquired.

"Ahem!"

Yes, he'd suspected trouble lay ahead. The throat clearing now confirmed the suspicion.

"I'm afraid I have bad news."

"No surprise there, my man."

Joseph frowned but didn't comment. "Since the most acute phase of your malady has passed, and we've seen to all urgent mine matters, I fear I must leave for an inexact length of time—but I should be back for Christmas."

Mervyn raised an eyebrow at the implied length of

Joseph's absence. "I do wish you'd come up with an exact length of time the next time you must leave. To vary the routine, you understand."

Joseph's frown deepened, and Mervyn fought to stifle a laugh.

"Well, you see, sir," the secretary said with extraordinary dignity, "it's about an emergency. How can a man ever gauge how long it might take to attend to one? Surely you do understand."

"This is hardly your first such emergency, my man. I've grown accustomed to your comings and goings."

The secretary wrung his hands. "But it truly is a matter of urgency, sir. I have a duty there, but I assure you, I would never think to shirk my duty to you, either. Still, I must indeed see to this situation."

Joseph's agitation, as always, was sincere.

Mervyn sighed and realized how often he did so around Joseph. The man seemed to invite much sighing and required great forbearance. "I do understand. I've never known you to be anything but responsible, and I suppose you do have a private life of some sort. I cannot imagine you to be any less responsible there."

"So may I have the time?"

"What good would it do me to deny you?"

Joseph's gray eyes widened. "Oh dear, Mr. Mervyn. You surely don't mean you've changed your mind and have decided to keep me here, do you?"

"Of course not. I've yet to deny a needy soul. And if you aren't the epitome of one—at least at this moment—then I don't know what one is."

"Thank you, Mr. Mervyn. I do thank you from the bottom of my heart."

In a whirl of paper and brown flannel, Joseph fled the room. Mervyn laughed out loud. Joseph's pattern of behavior was so regular, or perhaps it was more that Joseph and his doings were so regularly irregular, that Mervyn couldn't fault the man this time. He did, however, wonder.

What did Joseph do while he took off to see to one of his "emergencies"?

He sighed—again. He doubted he would ever know.

Chapter 1

That's a lovely portrait, Miss Meggie-moo," Rhiannon told her little cousin. "Now, how would you like to tell me who is in it?"

The strawberry-blond child nodded and smiled. "This one's Mama"—she pointed at one stick-and-blob figure with a great deal of plum stuff smeared over it—"and this one's Papa"—this one had gray instead of the plum—"and these are we."

The "we" wore splotches of various shades over their irregular physiques, but they all shared one characteristic. None could be recognized in any way. But that might be expected when the artist was a whopping five years of age.

"You are one very talented miss," Rhiannon declared. Meggie beamed.

Rhiannon gave the girl a one-armed hug. Gwynneth, Meggie's younger sister, lay sprawled over Rhiannon's other arm, her expression angelic despite her earlier bout of fretfulness. It seemed the baby was in the miserable process of cutting teeth, and nothing short of absolute exhaustion appeared to help soothe her.

"Are you gonna hold 'er like that all day?" demanded Dafydd, the fiery, carrot-orange-haired three-year-old. "I wanna build a fortress."

"It seems to me, young man, that time has come for your afternoon nap."

"Nooooooo. . ."

The boy ran toward the nursery door, but Meggie tackled him around the ankles and the two tumbled to the floor in a wild tangle of arms, legs, and giggles.

Rhiannon laughed. Without rousing the sleeping eighteen-month-old, she stood and took the baby to her crib. She tucked a whisper-soft wool blanket around the sturdy body, ran a finger over the silky cheek, and hurried back to the free-for-all in the other room.

She clapped her hands, but the two continued in their puppylike play. A smile curved her lips. The little scamps had stolen her heart the moment she'd laid eyes on them at birth. She'd always wished for younger siblings, but the Lord hadn't blessed her parents with any other children.

And then, when she turned sixteen, her mother died of influenza. Papa had been inconsolable and Rhiannon couldn't stem her own tears, much less help him. Her father had, of course, been in no condition to care for a young lady, especially since he bore all the burden of running his mine.

Just three months before Mama went to meet her Lord in heaven, Auntie Deirdre had married. Everyone expected her and Uncle Owen to have children immediately, so it was decided that Rhiannon should live with the newlyweds as they awaited the blessed arrivals. That way, she'd be ready to help her aunt, whose health had always been considered delicate, at the appropriate time.

But the Lord didn't see fit to bless her aunt and uncle with children for another three years. During that time, Rhiannon became educated, and she and her young aunt had become the dearest of friends, almost inseparable. Then the stream of rambunctious little cousins flowed forth. Rhiannon loved every single moment she spent with the children.

But enough was enough. "Come along, you two. It's time for a nice, long nap now. Go on—to bed with you both. Cousin Rhiannon has loads to do this afternoon."

The usual grumbles followed, but Rhiannon remained firm. After a few more minutes of the expected wheedling, the children marched off to their beds. Rhiannon ran downstairs, hoping Auntie Deirdre felt well enough to have tea downstairs instead of up in bed.

She found her father's much-younger sister in the parlor, a tufted footstool under her swollen ankles.

"I'm so glad to see you here!" Rhiannon hugged the lovely blond. "Is today a better day for you?"

"The nausea isn't as fierce as it's been," Deirdre said, relief in her voice. "But these ankles—I now know quite well how a sausage feels."

"Oh, Auntie, I'm so sorry for all this."

Deirdre smiled. "Just think of the blessing at the end of my time. That is all I'll let myself consider."

"And rich blessings your little ones are, too." The pillow under Deirdre's right arm seemed flat, so Rhiannon reached down to adjust it. "That pillow doesn't look very comfortable," she said. "Let me fluff it up for you."

Deirdre smiled, Rhiannon fluffed, and the two women discussed details of the meals for the following week.

A short while later, Mrs. Llewellyn, the Wylies' housekeeper, came into the pleasant room. " 'Fraid I must interrupt. We've a stranger at the door, here to see Miss Rhiannon, he says."

Rhiannon frowned. "A stranger? A *man*? Me?"

The dour housekeeper nodded.

"Goodness!" Deirdre exclaimed. "Who could it be?"

Mrs. Llewellyn shrugged. "Won't know if you don't go see."

Many times over the years, Rhiannon had longed to have a private chat with the sometimes insolent woman. But because the housekeeper did run the house so smoothly, she'd refrained from speaking out about the unpleasant attitude. Today, with Deirdre so beset by the troubles of pregnancy, she was again sorely tempted. She bit her tongue, however, and waited until Mrs. Llewellyn returned to her kingdom in the kitchen.

Deirdre tried to rise.

"Oh no, you don't, my dear," Rhiannon chided. "Don't even give it a thought. I'll take care of this matter myself. And it shouldn't take long. I can't imagine what anyone would want with me."

"Be careful, Rhiannon. You never know who might concoct an odd ruse with which to distract you. He may have evil motives, you know."

"I understand, Auntie, but I also know the Lord goes with me wherever I go. He'll fight my battle for me."

"If you wish, you can show the gentleman here into the parlor. There's always safety in numbers."

"If I feel the need, I surely will."

In the entry, the closed front door surprised her. Mrs. Llewellyn's blatant disdain of Rhiannon's caller made her chuckle—laughing was better than letting irritation rule. The woman did have a way about her, one Rhiannon didn't understand, much less appreciate, but she preferred to view matters in a humorous light whenever possible.

She opened the heavy wooden door. "Joseph!"

Her father's—exactly what *was* Joseph? Her father's secretary? Valet? Manservant? What did Joseph do?

Oh, it didn't matter, did it? "What—"

"Hello, Miss Rhiannon."

"What are you doing here in Cardiff?"

"Ahem!" He yanked off his hat and twirled the plain brown head topper in his hands by the brim. "I—ah— had business here. How are you, miss?"

Rhiannon knew all too well about Joseph's tendency

to come and go—mostly go—as he wished. He often left Papa in a bind at the mine office.

"I'm fine, as you can see for yourself." She couldn't get him to meet her gaze, and so she feared the worst. "Is—is Papa well? Oh, please tell me he's not—not. . ."

"Goodness, Miss Rhiannon! Don't even entertain such a notion. Your papa is. . .as well as can be expected."

"Joseph! Speak and tell me the truth. I beg you. You've never been one for half answers and vague ramblings. Don't start now. What is wrong with Papa?"

"Well. . .Mr. Mervyn *is* beset by another episode of gout, miss. He is in. . .*some* pain. Gout is a painfully miserable condition."

"Oh dear. I'm afraid I don't know much about it, Joseph. I do know Papa has these spells every so often. Is it serious?"

"Well, miss, the pain does fell him. He must take to bed and becomes quite incapacitated by the disease."

"Incapacitated!" Rhiannon's pulse pounded in her temples. "Why didn't you send for me? Why didn't you fetch me sooner?"

Again Joseph averted his gaze. "You must know what an unassuming man your dear papa is. He would never wish to impose on you—"

"How can you say that? Papa would never impose on me. I'd consider it an honor and a matter of love to care for him."

A strange, satisfied smile burst onto his face. "As I told him you would at each of the previous occasions. But he feels that to alert you to his medical woes would only trouble you with his misfortune. And, of course, he always mentions your fear of the mine as a reason to leave you be."

Guilt brought tears to Rhiannon's eyes. "Does he think I'd be so selfish as to put my fear before him?" A sob rose to her throat. "Oh, Joseph. Please tell me this isn't so."

For a moment, distress seemed to flit over Joseph's nondescript features. Then the slender man squared his bony shoulders and met her gaze. "He entertains no such notion, Miss Rhiannon. Still, I knew you'd want to know just how the man is faring. After all, you've always been a good Christian girl, and the dear Lord does call children to honor their parents."

"Oh, I do, I do, Joseph." She dabbed at her eyes with her lace hanky then squared her own shoulders. "My mind is made up. Even though Auntie Deirdre is in a bit of a difficult time, she does have Uncle Owen. Oh, and Mrs. Llewellyn, too, in spite of her temperament. Papa has no one."

"Ahem!" Joseph tipped his chin upward. "He does have me, miss."

"Of course, Joseph. But it's just not the same thing. I'm his daughter, and you—you're his—his. . ."

"Precisely!" He tugged his lapels straight. "So what is your plan, Miss Rhiannon?"

"Goodness, Joseph! I have scarcely learned the news, and you want me to have a plan ready-made?" She shook her head. "Aside from going to his side, I'm not sure what I'll do. I suppose I'll figure it out as I go."

He didn't seem satisfied, but Rhiannon couldn't do a thing about that. Right now, she had packing to do, a delicate aunt to upset with the news about her brother, sweet children to sadden at the departure of their adult playmate, and her own comfortable routine to disrupt.

But it was all for a worthwhile cause. Papa needed her. Even if he still lived near the mouth of that murderous hole in the ground. She would have to trust God to keep underground accidents at bay. She could never bear to witness the grief and turmoil the families of the miners suffered with each loss.

And there was—

But no, she couldn't think about *him*.

Why did God have to let tragedies happen? They touched so much. Even the heart and hopes of a young girl—the young girl she'd been when she vowed never to return to the village. Tragedy touched even the choices she made later in life.

She feared it always would.

Chapter 2

Rhiannon didn't know quite what to think when she walked out of Papa's room. She'd arrived only a scant fifteen minutes earlier and had rushed to see him. She'd expected to find him wan and racked by the pain. Instead, she'd seen the same Papa she always saw, a robust, hearty man, rosy-cheeked and cheerful, if indeed sore from the gout.

He, in turn, had been stunned to see her. Happy, yes, but stunned nonetheless. She never liked to think the worst of others, but she had to wonder if Joseph had lied to her about Papa's condition. He wasn't in agony, much less on his deathbed, as Joseph's vague hints and evasiveness had suggested.

Rhiannon had found his behavior odd for the usually straightforward if not blunt man, and in light of Papa's real condition, she found it outright bizarre.

She leaned against the bedroom door. The house was familiar, and she felt as though she'd wrapped a warm, comfortable blanket around her. But the village...

Arriving had brought back memories she'd tried hard to suppress. But she hadn't been able to do so. They'd come at her with a life all their own. As she'd ridden in the carriage, she'd tried not to look out at the cottages that filled the village. Many of them sheltered miner families, and too many of those families had lost loved ones in the mine.

That accursed hole in the ground.

Her stomach roiled just at the thought. The sound of the widows' wails, the sobs of the orphans it created, rang in her heart. How could anyone with any sense go down there? How could any woman tie herself to a man who did that kind of work day after day after day? How could anyone live with the risk?

Over all the normal sounds inside the family home, and despite its thick walls, she could still hear the pumping of the machines that made the colliery work. They emitted a relentless pulsation, and it felt to her the beats counted out the number of men whose lives it had taken, those men whose lives it had yet to take.

It wasn't loud, but rather hushed, like death itself.

"Well, hello there!"

The deep male voice startled her back from her somber thoughts. Rhiannon looked up and couldn't prevent a gasp.

"Tre–Trefor?"

"Indeed. And you must be my little friend Rhiannon, all grown up."

The light in his warm brown eyes reflected more than memories of the young girl who'd tagged along behind him. She suspected her own eyes were full of appreciation for her champion and hero. He seemed to like what he saw.

To her dismay, she liked what she could see, as well. Tall and broad-shouldered, Trefor resembled the youth she remembered in the clean-cut lines of his attractive features, the curve of his smile, and the confident way he carried himself. The former, however, had been a boy. This was a man.

"Cat nab your tongue, then?" he asked, humor in his words.

"Silence surely is unusual for me, don't you think?"

"There is a truth, indeed."

His gaze never left her face, and Rhiannon felt her cheeks go hot. *Arrrghh!* Her fair skin would reveal every hint of her discomfort. But there was nothing she could do about it.

Before she could respond, Trefor asked, "What would be bringing you back? I understood you'd vowed, back when you were all of sixteen, that you'd never be setting foot in the village again."

Rhiannon shrugged. "Circumstances change. Papa is ill. I felt the need to be at his side."

Trefor looked puzzled. "But this isn't his first spell of gout. And you've never troubled yourself to return before."

Her blush turned fiery. "And just who made you judge of my choices, Trefor Davies?"

"Not judging, I am. Just repeating what I've heard."

She still sensed the sting of judgment. "And what is it to you if I come or go? My father does understand me."

"We're all after understanding your fears, and everyone respects the dangers in the mine, but we cannot comprehend why you'd be leaving your father and your home. It's not as if you've ever needed to deal with the mine itself."

"Does compassion count for nothing with you? I've seen too many women and children torn to shreds by the pain of their loss. My own mother never forgot the loss of her father and brother. I cannot bear to see more of that."

Trefor's expression changed, but Rhiannon couldn't quite read what it revealed. Then he asked, "What is making this spell of gout so much different from the others? Why did you rush to your father's side this time when you didn't before?"

"No one ever bothered to let me know before. Joseph showed up at my auntie Deirdre's home—surprised me, to tell you true—told me Papa was ailing, and so here I am."

"So here you are. And will you be staying this time?"

Rhiannon couldn't contain the shudder. "Only so long as it takes for Papa to be back on his feet. Auntie Deirdre needs me in Cardiff. Her newest babe is due to arrive just after Christmas."

Trefor's lips pressed tight. "I see."

Rhiannon felt like stamping her foot, but she was no longer the young girl who'd followed him and fought against being dismissed by him and his friends. "I doubt you do see, but it's not for you to see, is it?"

He seemed ready to object but then changed his mind. "Will you be spending the Christmas holidays here at home, or will you be running away to Cardiff again?"

"Will you close down the colliery?"

"That is not what my job would be calling me to do. It's only your father who can be making that decision. But I heartily hope not."

"Why ever not? Do you want more men to die?"

Anger flared in his eyes. "Of course not, Rhiannon. But the men make a good wage in the mine. It's decent, honorable work that feeds and supports all those families. What would you be having them do if the mine were closed?"

She couldn't answer, so she chose the coward's way, and she knew she did just that. She changed the topic. "What brings you here today?"

He gave her a wry smile. "The mine. I'm after having my daily meeting with your father."

Rhiannon's stomach lurched. "So you really are a miner."

"And proud of it, Rhiannon. Don't you be forgetting that."

She really wished he'd chosen a different line of work. The interest she'd seen in his gaze matched the interest she felt. Not to mention that it brought back to life all the girlish feelings of adolescent love she'd once held for him.

She shook her head to dislodge the troublesome thoughts. "Ah—what do you do for Papa?"

"I'm his superintendent."

The groan slipped past her lips. "So you're responsible for the well-being and safety of the men."

He again shrugged. "I'm told I do a good job."

"I don't doubt it. But you're in and out of that pit."

"Daily."

"I see." The chat had gone on long enough. At least for her it had. "Well, Mr. Davies, it's been interesting to meet you again."

"Rhiannon?" he said in a soft voice. "Don't be forgetting the most important thing."

"What would that be?"

"The Lord goes with us into the mine, just as He goes with us to chapel on Sunday mornings."

"Then why would He leave you to die in the pit?"

He shook his head, a sad look on his face, nodded farewell, and then went into Papa's room.

A pity. Such a splendid man wasted and in danger deep in a hole in the earth.

What was it about that prickly redhead that still had a hold on him? Trefor shook his head. He'd been unable— or perhaps more truthfully, unwilling—to shoo her away when they were younger; and now, all these years later, he'd let her under his skin, let her rile him.

"Well?" Mervyn Gwynne asked. "Will you stay standing there like a statue, man?"

Trefor shook his head. " 'Tis is sorry I am, sir. If you'll forgive me, I can be telling you about today's work."

Trefor gave his employer a clear, concise listing of the day's accomplishments and the mine's output. As usual, Mervyn complimented him on a job well done, and Trefor thanked the older man. Then, as he was about to open the door to leave, Mervyn called his name.

"Yes, sir?"

"I heard you speaking to my daughter as you came in. I do remember you always had a soft spot in your heart for my little girl, how you let her shadow you when boys your age would have sent her packing instead. What do you think of how Rhiannon has grown?"

A pang of alarm shot through Trefor. What could

he tell his employer about the man's daughter? That she had always been an appealing child and had become the loveliest woman Trefor had ever seen? That he'd always had Rhiannon's memory tucked in the farthest corner of his mind? That on one or two absolutely mad occasions, he'd dared think of dangerous possibilities?

Of course not. So he blurted out, "She's certainly bigger."

Mervyn laughed. "I hardly think Rhiannon would see that as flattering."

Trefor was glad for the lowered lighting in the room. He didn't want Mervyn to see the mortification on his face. "That isn't what I was meaning, sir. But she is no longer a child."

Mervyn's eyes danced. "And she's a fine young Christian woman, well educated, gifted in the care of children, and helps run my sister's home like a fine-tuned clock. A true gem for any wise man."

Why did Trefor feel like a hound at the rear of a hunt?

He edged closer to the door. "Sure I am that she is."

"Only a fool would let her go."

"Ah—certainly."

"I'm glad you're no fool, man. You do an excellent

job for me. I'm proud to call you friend."

That was enough. "Heading home I should be, sir. I've practice tonight."

"For the *eisteddfod*, right?" When Trefor nodded, the door knob in his hand, Mervyn went on. "Good, good. It shall be a pleasure to hear you sing, then."

Not even the nervousness that beset Trefor each time he stood in front of an adjudicator during the traditional competition could rival the flurries of agitation he felt right now. He gave Mervyn a final nod in farewell, pulled the door shut, and left.

What did Rhiannon's return have to do with him?

More to the point, why would Mervyn ask the questions he had?

If Trefor didn't know better, he'd be thinking the older man had something in mind. Something that was never meant to be.

Mervyn dropped back onto his pillows. He chuckled. Pity Margot hadn't lived to see the results of his nudging. She would have had herself a good laugh, too.

That girl of theirs—she'd yet to bother herself with finding a man she would love and cherish and who would care for her. She wasn't so young anymore.

And Trefor Davies? A better man, Mervyn didn't know.

"That was splendid, sir," Joseph said as he extricated himself from within the bowels of Mervyn's large wardrobe. "The boy isn't totally dense, and he should know to take the lead from here."

"Oh, Trefor Davies is anything but dense, and he knows perfectly well what my questions meant. I just have to wonder if perhaps my nudging won't make him react in the opposite way than we want."

Joseph tugged down his coat sleeves. "I shouldn't give it much thought, sir. It's inevitable. Anyone with eyes can see they're each other's perfect match. They might perhaps lack a certain vision, a large enough measure of discernment. The Lord surely blesses those who seek discernment. One can only hope these two find it as they mature. Goodness knows they're ripe enough already."

Mervyn shot his secretary a pointed look. "You speak of them as though they were apples hanging from a tree."

"One can see them as fruit, sir, sown by the Lord, tended by Trefor's parents, you, your sadly mourned wife, and your dear sister. I'd say they're now ready for the picking, if one might be so bold to say."

"Picking?"

"Of course. Picking as in picking a mate, as in picking one who will answer a call, as in picking one who will carry on a legacy of faith and tradition."

Sometimes Joseph's way of speaking left Mervyn dizzy. This line of thought threatened to do just that. "I don't quite see what Trefor and Rhiannon have to do with answering calls and carrying on legacies. I just want my daughter married, and I'm wanting me a fistful of grandchildren."

"Oh, you shall have them, sir. You shall. In due time."

Then the maddening fellow opened the door and headed out.

"Joseph!" Mervyn called. "What are you up to now?"

Joseph glanced back and, to Mervyn's eternal shock, gave him an impish wink.

Winking? Impish? *Joseph?*

"I'm off to see about some reaping," the secretary then said.

Mervyn dropped back onto his pillows, his thoughts in the usual swirl Joseph left in his wake.

When would he ever learn? It was always best to let Joseph just leave. He knew he really shouldn't try to extract answers from the bewildering man.

Joseph was Joseph, unpredictable, mysterious, and quite exasperating. But all too often, he also happened to make a great deal of sense.

Even when Mervyn couldn't quite discern it.

Chapter 3

Two days after her initial meeting with Trefor, Rhiannon lingered too long over tea in Papa's room. Trefor arrived as she was gathering Papa's plate and silverware.

He seemed as surprised to see her there as she was to be caught by his entrance.

"I can return later," he told Papa.

"Nonsense, my man, nonsense. After all, you and Rhiannon are great friends from long ago. What could be more pleasant than to chat among friends?"

"Oh, but I wouldn't want to interrupt business," she said. "I'll be back in a while with that book you wanted."

"What's the hurry, Rhiannon?" Papa asked, his cheer a mite overdone. "Have a seat, both of you. It's grand to pause for a moment of rest at the end of a long day, Trefor."

Rhiannon perched at the foot of the bed, the tray at her side on top of the wool blanket. Trefor took the large armchair where Papa liked to sit and read.

Looks were exchanged.

The silence grew thick and uncomfortable.

"Ahem!"

Everyone turned to the door.

Joseph smiled. "A tea party, I see."

Trefor snorted.

Rhiannon gaped.

Out of the corner of her eye, she saw Papa's face turn ruddy, and then he coughed.

Joseph seemed oblivious to everyone's response. "Just exactly what Miss Rhiannon should be up to on a regular basis. If only a wise man would step up and make her his honorable wife."

Her mortification knew no bounds. "Joseph!"

"Would you agree with my dear sister, Deirdre, and me," Papa said to Trefor, "that with all her accomplishments and her beauty, Rhiannon should have gentlemen queued up to seek her hand in holy matrimony?"

She turned to that traitor. "Papa!"

Trefor squirmed in the large chair.

Joseph marched into the center of the room. "And although you and your lovely lady wife weren't blessed with a large brood," he said to Mervyn, "I'm certain Miss Rhiannon will make a fine breeder."

Rhiannon wailed and rose; the silver and china clinked.

Mervyn chuckled. "If you have any doubts, just take look at Deirdre, will you? She'll be having her fourth in a few months."

Fire in her belly, Rhiannon glared. "How could you both be so horrid to me? Have you no shame? You've certainly shamed me in front of Trefor."

She ran from the room, slammed the door, and somehow made her way to the library, a sheet of tears blurring her vision. How could she ever forgive Papa and that— that ratty secretary or valet or whatever Joseph was?

Auntie Deirdre, Uncle Owen, and Papa had made no secret how they felt about Rhiannon's unwed state. She knew they wished to see her "settled" in a home of her own. Trouble was, none of Owen's friends had ever sparked the slightest twinkle of interest in her.

In fact, no man she'd ever met had managed to dim Trefor's memory. To her current regret.

She collapsed into the plump settee in the far corner of the library. One thing was certain; she could never face Trefor again. Not after the disastrous encounter in the room of that meddling matchmaker father of hers.

Rhiannon sniffled into her linen handkerchief. What a dreadful situation. But at least it proved one thing. She didn't belong back here in the village. Papa seemed more than well on the road to recovery. They certainly didn't need her. First thing in the morning, she'd call that rat Joseph and have him ready the carriage for her.

She simply had to return to Cardiff.

"Oh!"

Rhiannon sat up at the soft cry. "Who's there?"

"Are you well, Miss Rhiannon?" asked Ceridwen, the new maid. "I'm after the book I—ah—well, you see, it's that I'm fond of reading, and I found a book here—"

"Help yourself," Rhiannon said. "I'm a great reader, too."

"But you weren't here for reading, were you now?"

She sighed. "No. I had to compose myself."

"It's surprised I am to find you like this. What is the matter?"

Rhiannon didn't think she could make the village girl understand. But she felt the need to talk, to let her feelings out. "I don't belong here, Ceridwen—"

"Everyone calls me Ceri, Miss Gwynne."

"And everyone calls me Rhiannon, Ceri. Please do."

"That I couldn't be doing, miss. Miss Rhiannon—will that do?"

"It'll be fine." She took a deep breath. "Papa and Joseph and Auntie Deirdre have this notion that I need to marry, and soon. It troubles them to think I might be unhappy as a spinster. But I'm not unhappy, not as unhappy as I'd be if—"

Ceri's blue eyes narrowed. "If what?"

"If I married the wrong man just for the sake of wedding."

"Would you be having a 'right' man you'd rather marry?"

Rhiannon couldn't stop the blush. "Not really."

"Ah—it sounds like you've been struggling with yourself."

"No, not me. It's just that his life isn't one I can live." Rhiannon knew she shouldn't speak so openly, but at the moment she couldn't help herself. Ceri seemed interested, and she also seemed perceptive. "Are you married?"

Ceri nodded. "Only six months."

"Who's your husband?"

"Phillip Roberts," she said, stars in her eyes. "He's a fine man, and a good worker at the mine."

"Oh." Rhiannon didn't know what more to say.

The silence grew.

Ceri frowned. "Do you know him? Are you disliking him? I assure you, Phil is a hard worker and kind and decent."

"Oh, Ceri, I don't know your Phil, and I'm certain he's all you say he is. It's just that—well, you see—he's a miner."

The blue eyes opened wide. "Ah, I see. And you are fearing the mine, then."

"An unreasonable fear," Trefor said from the door. "But I am understanding it. And also why you left your father's room."

"You must see now why I don't belong here. The mine is bad enough. But then Papa. . ." She shook her head. "And we can't forget that—that troublemaker Joseph. Goodness! He's as dreadful as Papa."

Trefor winced. "Heavy-handed they were."

Rhiannon squared her shoulders. "You'd best run, Trefor. You might find yourself hog-tied and wed if you don't. Those two are a frightening force."

Alarm looked comical on Trefor's face, but Rhiannon was in no mood for humor. She headed for the door. "You can come or you can go as you please, Trefor Davies. It's your business what work you do and how often you meet with my father. As for me, I'll be leaving first thing in the morning. Papa is well enough, and Auntie Deirdre and the children do, indeed, need me. I refuse to stay here until the next mine disaster comes about."

"But, Miss Rhiannon!"

She stopped and glanced at the young woman. "But what?"

"What about our dear Lord? Are you forgetting Him? He's our Protector, our Guide, our Father who loves us and who'll never leave us or forsake us!"

"He's forsaken those who go into the depths of that pit." She drew a deep breath. "Call me weak, if you must. But I cannot see spending the rest of my life worried over what I'll find at the pithead, remembering what my mother went through when her father and brother died down there. I could never bring a child into a life like that, one where the Lord could forget that child's father deep inside the ground."

Trefor made a noise deep in his throat. "I can see that your mind is made up. You'll not be listening to reason. Good evening, Miss Gwynne. It's been—interesting, meeting up with you yet again."

Rhiannon blinked. He'd tossed the words she'd spoken back at her. *Hmm. . .*

"Back home to my Phillip I'll be heading, Miss Rhiannon," Ceri murmured. Then, before she left the room, she added, "Right your father and auntie might be, worried about you. I'm not liking the mine any more than you, but I'd rather be living with faith in God and at my Phil's side than all alone but for that cold, cold fear."

Ceri's words pierced deep. Rhiannon was alone; she'd felt that way even in the midst of the bustle at Auntie Deirdre's very full home, no matter how much she loved her aunt and the children, no matter how much they loved her. Was she ready to face an empty future?

And why should Trefor care so much how she felt about the mine? Did he—could he possibly be in with Papa and Joseph in their tiresome meddling? Could the interest she thought she'd seen in his eyes have meant something?

Surely not.

And had Ceri meant to say that Rhiannon's faith was lacking? True, she couldn't trust that the mine wouldn't explode, cave in, and kill more men. How could she trust the God who'd let that happen so many times before?

"He wasn't any happier than she was, was he?" Mervyn mused.

Joseph shook his head. "Perhaps we did push her a bit far."

"But they're stubborn and blind." Mervyn felt another cough build up in his chest. "Please fetch me some fresh water, Joseph. I've been fighting a wretched tickle in my throat all day."

The secretary left the room, and Mervyn tried to get comfortable in his bed. He was more than tired of his bed. He'd been feeling fairly well of late, but once Rhiannon arrived, he'd realized that the only way to keep her in the village was to continue his recovery at a slower pace than it truly called for.

He was heartily sick of pillows and blankets and the boredom of his room. He wanted to return to his office, return to his men.

But he had a duty to see his daughter settled, and he

wouldn't let up until that day came to pass.

Joseph walked in and set a pitcher of cool water on the small chest at the right side of Mervyn's bed. "Here you are, Mr. Mervyn."

"Thank you." He took a deep drink then met his friend and secretary's gaze. "Do you think we went too far?"

"You know as well as I do that the good Lord has a plan for His children."

"Of course I know that. And as far as that daughter of mine and my superintendent are concerned, that future is one full of the love and joy that come with a family."

"I couldn't agree with you more."

Mervyn's cough lasted longer this time than the last. "I'm afraid I've come down with some silly new—thing. And just when we're making progress with Rhiannon and Trefor."

"It's just as well that you're abed and stay there, sir."

Mervyn smiled. "I like the way you think, Joseph. Oh, indeed, there will be love and joy for Trefor and Rhiannon. And the grandbabies will be for me to spoil."

Joseph nodded sagely. "And we'll trust the Father to

deal with Miss Rhiannon's extraordinary fear—"

"Unreasonable fear, you mean."

Joseph shrugged. "In either case, we'll have to trust the Father to heal her fear of the mine."

"The only thing that keeps our lovely future at bay."

Chapter 4

Trefor wished Rhiannon hadn't come back. During the time she'd been gone, he'd worked to persuade himself that his feelings for her years ago had been only those of a childhood friend. But at the back of his mind, one detail always remained. Rhiannon, at sixteen, had been the same age some village girls were when they married or even bore children.

And he'd been working in the mine for a while by then; at eighteen he'd done the work of a man, just like any other miner.

Still, he'd tried. And he'd almost succeeded. Until he saw her in the hall the other day. Then he'd known he'd always have strong feelings for Rhiannon Gwynne, and it didn't matter how much effort he put in to change that fact.

His feelings had nothing to do with her natural beauty. The silky, golden-red curls and green eyes were wonderful to look at, as were the delicate face and her feminine figure, but what most caught his eye was the vibrant energy that seemed to surround her. She made him think of a magnet. He was the helpless bit of steel.

He feared he wouldn't be able to resist her appeal if she stayed much longer. And losing his heart to her would be a terrible mistake.

She hadn't overcome her fear of the mine.

He still was a miner.

How could those two facts ever be reconciled?

As always when a problem seemed too great, Trefor turned to God for strength, wisdom, and guidance. He fell to his knees and prayed.

And not just once.

He prayed often and would continue to pray until the good Lord saw fit to give him the answers to the questions he'd asked today.

When Rhiannon went to bid her father good-bye early

the next day, she carried with her a certain amount of fear. She didn't want to see the disappointment on her father's face when he realized she wouldn't stay. She also didn't want to discuss her fear of the mine.

But what met her when she entered the room sparked fear much greater than what she'd brought with her. Papa was ill. Much more so than even when she'd first arrived.

Papa's eyes watered, his cheeks burned red, his breath wheezed, and when he tried to speak, a fit of coughing cut off the words before they even began.

The fever, the rough breaths, and the misery he obviously felt took Rhiannon back a number of years. Yes, she'd been young then, but nothing would make her forget her mother's fight against a particularly virulent case of the influenza. In a short time, Mama had lost her fight.

Papa couldn't die; he just couldn't.

Of course, she wouldn't even think again of a return to Cardiff, at least not until Papa was back on his feet. Auntie Deirdre would make out well enough with the help of her housekeeper and husband, and surely the three of them would find a young woman to take Rhiannon's place.

She, on the other hand, couldn't leave Papa's care in the hands of the unpredictable and mysterious Joseph. What did he know of nursing? Would he even know to call a doctor to see to Papa's care?

She doubted he would. So she simply had to stay.

She'd deal with her feelings—for the mine, as well as those for the mine superintendent—once she had her father back on the road to health.

"Joseph!" she called out the door. "Please come to Papa's room. I need your help."

Not only did Joseph run in, but Ceri also appeared, her fair skin flushed, her blond hair bouncing in its knot atop her head. Mrs. Devane, the Gwynnes' longtime housekeeper, followed, hampered by her generous girth and advancing age.

"What is wrong?" Joseph asked as he came to a stop.

"Papa's ill—again!"

"Oh dear!" Ceri cried. "What would you be needing for him, miss? How can I be helping you?"

"Goodness gracious!" Mrs. Devane clucked. "Mr. Mervyn, I was warning you the other day. That walk you were taking to that office of yours downstairs didn't do you much good."

Rhiannon frowned. "I thought he'd been abed for weeks."

"He had," the plump lady said. "Needing his papers, he was saying. As if a paper would be doing him any good."

Papa pushed himself up on one elbow. "All of you," he said, his voice a croak, "take your blathering somewhere else! Can't a man get a minute's rest here?"

Another series of coughs punctuated his peevish words. Then he fell back onto the pillows, rolled over, and closed his eyes.

"I need to feel useful," he added with a shiver, as if chilled.

Rhiannon gestured the others from the room. "You'll be far more useful if you take the time to truly get well." She tucked the blanket around his shoulders. "I'll come back with some tea and toast in a bit. Rest now."

She dropped a kiss on his head then left the room. The others had waited for her in the hall. Although she'd never dealt with anything more serious than the occasional nursery upset tummy and sniffles and scrapes, Rhiannon knew she had to act.

"Joseph, I need you to fetch Papa's doctor. I don't

think old Dr. Gruffud is still available, is he?"

"No, but his son, young Dr. Gruffud, would be happy to come. He's been treating your papa's gout."

"Then please go fetch him." To the two women, she said, "We'll be needing plenty of plain food, easy for him to eat. I should think his throat hurts from all those coughs."

Mrs. Devane nodded, lines drawn by worry on her brow. "Not liking the looks of him, Miss Rhiannon."

"I'm not, either. Reminds me of—"

"Of your dear mama, all those years ago."

Rhiannon nodded. Her eyes burned with tears that threatened to spill. But she couldn't let them. She had Papa to think of. His health had to come before anything else.

She turned to the young maid. "Could you perhaps heat a stone for his feet, Ceri? Please watch that you wrap it well. We don't want to burn him."

"There is good, Miss Rhiannon. He will surely be sweating out the illness then."

Rhiannon only nodded. If only influenza were a matter of sweating out a bit of a cold. It was a serious disease, one that had killed, even those who had been healthy and well before it struck its nasty blow, and the gout had weakened Papa.

She wrote a brief note to her aunt, alerting her of Rhiannon's uncertain return date. Joseph took the envelope with him when he went after Dr. Gruffud.

The wait for their arrival proved more difficult than Rhiannon would have thought. She found refuge in Papa's office with a good book and warm blanket, since the weather had turned colder overnight.

The doctor's diagnosis didn't surprise her. Papa did, indeed, have influenza. Everyone in the household was at risk. They could all come down with the dread disease, but Papa would still need care. Rhiannon knew it wouldn't be easy, but she promised the doctor she would do her best.

Papa had fallen asleep by the time the doctor left. Rhiannon returned to the office, but this time, the book did nothing to hold her attention. Although she tried to pray, her fears and the memories of Mama stole any vestige of peace she might have found. As the sun was setting, Ceri came into the room and lit a fire in the broad hearth.

"You surely will be catching the influenza if you put off caring for yourself," she chided Rhiannon. "Much good you'll be doing your papa then."

"Thank you, Ceri. You're right. The room is chilly, even though I hadn't noticed. I wrapped myself in my wool blanket and spent hours trying to pray."

A wise pair of blue eyes assessed her. "Thinking yourself sick is silly, right?"

She sighed. "You're right. But I feel the Lord's left me. I don't think He hears me pray."

Ceri hurried to Rhiannon's side. "Having to help you with that, me."

The young woman took Rhiannon's icy hand and, in a soft voice, led them in a loving conversation with their Lord.

The opening door interrupted their prayers.

"Sorry I am," Trefor said. "I didn't realize anyone was here."

Rhiannon turned aside and wiped her tears with a quick flick of her hand. She didn't want him to see her weep.

"Did you come to see my father?" she asked, wrapping herself in her pink blanket again.

"Wanting to talk to him about the mine like every other day," he said.

Before Rhiannon could stop her, Ceri slipped out the door. She sighed. Perhaps this encounter with her childhood hero would go better than the last one had.

"Papa's taken ill again, Trefor. We had young Dr. Gruffud out here earlier. He said it was the influenza."

Trefor shook his head. "Not good—"

"Don't do that!" she cried. "Don't you be counting him for dead, Trefor Davies! I'm here, and I'm going to make sure he recovers."

Something lit his expression, and to Rhiannon it looked like admiration. *Oh my!*

"Good for you," he said. "But now I must be seeing him about the mine."

She crossed her blanket-covered arms as her anger began to rise. "Did you not hear what I just told you? Papa is ill. You are not taking into that room the worries and troubles of that miserable mine. How do you expect him to heal if you fill his head with all that?"

"That miserable mine, as you call it, is feeding a whole village full of families. It cannot just go idle, waiting for your papa to get well."

Rhiannon recognized the truth of Trefor's words. But she couldn't let him trouble her ailing father. "Very well. Because of those families, the mine must run. But I don't much care how it goes about it."

His red cheekbones said she'd piqued his temper.

"You would be caring if it meant the next meal on your children's table."

"Then if you're so passionate about the murderous thing, run it yourself. Surely as Papa's superintendent, you know what must be done. Go ahead. Do what needs done. Just don't be troubling Papa while he's abed."

He looked ready to argue but then seemed to think better of his initial impulse. "I still need information, and since it isn't mine to do as I wish, I can't be doing just anything I think of on my own. Decisions must be made—"

"You are an honorable man, Trefor," she said in a calmer voice. "I understand you don't want to overstep your bounds, but Papa—Papa could die if he doesn't get the rest he needs. I saw Mama die of this cursed disease. I'll do whatever I must to see that he doesn't do so, as well."

Trefor remained an unmovable wall.

Rhiannon took a deep breath. "Fine. If you're un-willing to make the decisions yourself, then have patience with me. I'll use whatever sense the Lord gave me and make those decisions until Papa can do so for himself again. I'll take all the responsibility myself."

The alarm on Trefor's face solidified her decision. "I know what you're thinking," she said. "You think I'm not capable of running the mine. But you're wrong."

Had she really said those words? Was she out of her mind? "Well, if you'll just give me a chance to understand what it takes to keep it running, I'll show you I can. With your experience in that hideous black hole and my common sense, I'm certain we'll do as well as Papa and you have done."

Had Rhiannon been an innocent bystander, and Trefor reacting to someone else's words, she surely would have found his increased horror humorous. But since it was directed at her and her earnest efforts, it only served to spur her along.

"I find your response insulting," she said on her way to the door. "And it's certainly far from humorous— should it be your feeble attempt at humor. And now, if you'll excuse me, I have a great deal I still must do."

She left the room, head high, shoulders firm, spine straight. Her exit would have been dignified and majestic had she not been swaddled in the silly pink blanket from her bed.

Instead of dignified, however, she only managed to look absurd. All those masses of thick, warm fabric got tangled around her ankles, so rather than glide away with grace, she lurched and staggered down the hall.

A male chuckle followed in her wake.

Chapter 5

Her intentions had been good. The results, however, weren't.

Trefor hadn't wanted to take over the mine operations, but when Rhiannon decided she would make the decisions he didn't dare make and her ailing father couldn't, he'd known he was in for a rough time.

He'd had no idea how rough.

To his every question, she'd replied, "What do you think?"

When he reminded her she'd agreed to decide, she'd said, "Very well. If you don't have any ideas, then you'll just have to shut down the mine. That's my decision."

In the end, she'd had her way—of sorts. He'd taken over the day-to-day running of her father's mine and made each and every decision needed. But Trefor had also won one minor victory. He'd made her listen to each one of his decisions, to every last trouble he'd encountered. His conscience had demanded that at least one Gwynne knew the workings of the mine.

Not that she'd cared. She'd focused all her attention on her father's health. And Trefor had been unable to fault her for that. He understood her love for Mervyn.

To Trefor's relief, Mervyn did begin to recover from his bout of influenza. As serious a disease as it was, it appeared the man would beat it. But not soon enough for Trefor. Especially since Mervyn wanted nothing to do with the business that, up until now, had meant more to him than anything but his daughter.

Now he wanted Trefor to run the colliery. Trefor couldn't understand the man's reasoning.

"Of course you can do it, my man," Mervyn insisted each time Trefor hesitated to take action without the older man's input. "You did quite well while I couldn't even raise my head. Besides, it's the perfect time for a younger man to take the reins. I'm getting old. All I want now is time to spend with Rhiannon and those grandchildren she'd better hurry and give me."

That bothered him more than just about anything else. Each time Mervyn mentioned grandchildren, Trefor felt walls close around him. Had he let his most private dreams and wishes show?

On the rare occasion Trefor had allowed himself to dream, he'd thought of a future with Rhiannon at his side. He'd also dreamed of children—red-haired little ones with green eyes and charming smiles.

But reality hadn't changed. Nothing more than friendship could exist between them. The woman Rhiannon had become would never accept the love of a man like Trefor, a miner through and through. As much as she loved her father, and despite Mervyn's love for his mine, she would never consider a future at the side of the man who'd worked hard with Mervyn to implement many improvements in the mine.

Trefor would never leave his village; he belonged here. He was certain Rhiannon accepted that as fact. Just as he accepted that, at some point in the coming days, she would leave. Rhiannon didn't belong here.

The sooner Mervyn recovered, the sooner the sweet temptation of Rhiannon's presence would be gone. The longer she stayed, the more Trefor feared falling in love.

Or perhaps he'd already done that a number of years ago. The feelings he'd believed nothing more than the foolishness of an adolescent lad seemed to have returned a thousandfold the day she came home.

But he couldn't let himself love Rhiannon. Not the way a man should love his wife, not with that forever kind of love. So he continued to seek God in prayer; he asked for the Lord's help time after time after time. He couldn't fight his love for the beautiful Rhiannon on his own. And that was a battle he had to win before she left the village again.

Otherwise, she'd leave his heart the true victim of her father's ill health.

If she had to face Trefor Davies one more time, she would surely go mad. Rhiannon could scarcely turn around in her own home without running into the man. Even though Papa was well on the way to a full recovery, he still couldn't return to work. He tired too easily, and a nagging little cough lingered.

Not that Rhiannon wanted him to deal with the mine again.

While everything about the colliery repelled her,

she knew some of her ideas had merit. But she'd wanted Trefor to make the decisions. She'd seen a spark of—was it ambition? Desire perhaps? Whatever it might be, she'd seen it in his eyes. And since Papa had repeated more times than she cared to count how little he was ready to do about the mine just yet, she'd wanted Trefor to have the opportunity to see how capable he could be.

She couldn't let herself love him, but she could give him a future that might keep him out of the mine. If he were to run the business aboveground, then perhaps the woman he eventually married wouldn't have to fear that hole in the ground as much as Rhiannon did.

She wished. . .

But no. Rhiannon couldn't stay. No matter what. The memories of her mother's suffering after the loss of her father and brother would never go away. But she could leave Trefor with a better future than the one her mother's loved ones had.

She only wished Papa's normally robust health would hurry up and return. She had to get back to Cardiff as soon as she could. Just as she'd feared, she could no longer deny her renewed feelings for the diligent, capable man Trefor had become.

And she feared that when she left, she'd be leaving her heart behind.

November took what felt like forever to end. Rhiannon hadn't expected to still be in the village when December arrived, but there she was, Papa still weak from his battle with influenza and unable, or perhaps unwilling, to return to work even now. Had his recent serious illness shown him how fragile life could be? Had that influenced his view of working the mine?

She didn't know, but she wished he'd take a step into the future, no matter what that future held.

The weather had turned bitter. Rhiannon wrapped her wool shawl tighter around her and looked out the office window at the mountains, their tops white with the snow that fell fresh all too often these days. The sun had set hours ago, and the moon now hung in the dark sky.

If she looked just to the right of the house and toward the far end of the valley, she could see the pile of rubble near the mouth of the mine. Snow might fall and cover it, but each day men went into the earth, dug for hours, brought out the good with the bad, and added more waste to yesterday's lot. The heap served to remind her of those who risked their lives underground, even when they'd left for the day and now took their rest in the safety of their homes.

Trefor. . .

Even though he still ran the colliery these days, Rhiannon knew he had gone inside on any number of occasions.

"Why?" she'd asked.

"Making sure the new uprights were put in right, I was."

The chill of fear pierced her to the bone. "You went in, not knowing if the uprights supporting the mine's roof were right? You knew there was a chance they might fail and the roof cave, but you still went in?"

"You'd be wanting me to send my men in without making sure they'd be safe? What kind of man would you be thinking me?"

"A sane one."

"A coward."

"Of course not. Just a reasonable man."

"How could the men I send underground be respecting me if they knew I wouldn't do the same?"

She had no argument then. She knew he was right,

but her fear remained. She had turned and left the room. He'd gone into her father's room, where they'd spent a long while engrossed in the business she. . .she hated.

There. She'd admitted it. She hated her father's mine. The place where the man she loved worked.

And she'd also admitted the truth of her feelings. She loved Trefor Davies. Heaven help her, since she could no longer help herself.

No matter what happened, today, tomorrow, next year—her heart would never be the same.

"Do you think we pushed too hard?" Mervyn asked Joseph after a distracted Trefor left his room. "I've been more than ready to leave this dreary room for days—no, weeks. And nothing. They still argue at every chance. Didn't you hear them before he came in here tonight?"

Joseph nodded. "Can't say for certain. But I have thought of something. I should perhaps leave for a while. That way Miss Rhiannon will be forced to do the office work she's tried to make Mr. Trefor do. She'd learn more about the colliery, of how you both work to improve the conditions and the safety of your men. Knowledge might help ease some of her fears."

Mervyn laughed. "Now there's your most inventive excuse to disappear as of yet, my man."

Joseph's expression grew even more serious. "But, Mr. Mervyn, it's the absolute truth. If she begins to work at his side—really work with him, not just shift all the work onto him—she'll see that while the colliery does have its risks, it isn't quite the man-killer she believes it to be. Besides, Mr. Trefor is a man of great faith. Perhaps he'll help her find hers again."

"It's too late now, Joseph. Perhaps you should have thought of that a week or two ago." Mervyn shook his head. "No. It's past time for me to leave this bed. Our plan is never going to work."

"Have patience," Joseph argued. "Just a little longer."

"I think you're mad, but I'll give you a few more days."

"Remember, Mr. Mervyn"—a twinkle appeared in Joseph's eyes—"there's nothing more romantic than Christmastime and all the lovely festivities that surround our celebration of the Lord's birth."

Mervyn laughed. "You are right there. Now if only we could get them to enjoy those festivities together. . . ."

"You must go in my place," Papa argued.

"But I know nothing of the local *eisteddfod*," Rhiannon wailed.

"You don't need to know much. You only need ears to listen and then enjoy. Besides, ours is more of a *cymanfa ganu*, a singing of hymns, than a true eisteddfod competition, where all sorts of poems and dances and songs are performed."

"But you said I needed to judge. I don't know enough about these hymns to be a fair judge—"

"You'd only be an honorary adjudicator," he cut in with a wave. "The real ones will carry the burden of deciding the winner of the singing festival."

Eventually, and with great misgivings, Rhiannon agreed to take Papa's place. And that's how she happened to be at the chapel two weeks before Christmas, seated just in front of the altar with the rest of the adjudicators.

To her surprise, she enjoyed every minute of the competition, the singing more than the few poems some had wanted to recite. Fortunately for her, her judging talents, meager as they were, would be needed only to decide the winner of the singers.

But just when she'd begun to relax, a new competitor took his place. Trefor waited until he was given the signal to start.

In Welsh rather than English, as was required at the event, his rich tenor voice flowed over Rhiannon in a way that differed from all that had come before. His song of praise rose and fell, and his love for God showed in the reverence on his face, the deep emotion in his voice.

To her dismay, Rhiannon had to acknowledge yet another trait that appealed to her. Trefor was hard-working, honest, brave—and now devout, as well. She wished she had the depth of faith he revealed with his hymn of praise. Maybe then she wouldn't feel the need to leave the village; maybe then she'd have the courage to see if what she'd thought she saw in his eyes that first day back was real.

A knot formed in her throat, and tears burned in her eyes. She loved the Lord. But did she dare. . . ? Could she really trust God? Could she leave her fears with Him and step forward into. . .*what*? What could God possibly have in store for her?

Deep inside, without making a sound, she prayed, *Father in heaven, I confess the boundaries I've put on my faith. I've let fear and cowardice rule. But I don't know how to change. How to have the kind of faith courage requires. I can't do it myself, but if You're the God of all, the King of kings, surely You can show me how—how to trust.*

Applause broke into her prayer. Her heart swelled with pride at the admiration everyone expressed for the man she loved. How she wished she were worthy of him.

But this wasn't the time to think that kind of thought. It was time to judge. And while Rhiannon tried to remain impartial, the one performer who deserved to win was—

"Mr. Trefor Davies!"

The chief adjudicator wore a broad smile as he congratulated the winner. Rhiannon's could be no less broad and bright. That night, images of Trefor filled her dreams, his voice again raised in earnest worship of his Lord.

The next day, Rhiannon spent the better part of the morning with Ceri. The two women cut, tied, and then hung bunches of mistletoe and branches of holly throughout the house. The scents and sights of the approaching holiday served to cheer Rhiannon in a way nothing else had as of yet.

"More mistletoe, Miss Rhiannon?" Ceri asked, a twinkle in her eyes.

"I'd say we've hung plenty all over the house."

"A kiss, you'll be after."

Despite all her efforts, Rhiannon blushed. "Not at all. Auntie Deirdre always fills her house with pretty greens, and I think Papa will appreciate the color when he finally comes down."

"Mmm. . ."

"I do mean it, Ceri. I can't wait for Papa to join me at the table again. And I want the house to feel as joyful and festive as possible."

A mischievous smile curved the maid's lips. "I'm after believing you."

Rhiannon didn't believe her, either, but she let the matter go. At least until later when she ran into Trefor as he walked out of Papa's room.

"Good evening, Rhiannon," he said.

"And to you." Then she added, "You were wonderful at the eisteddfod. I was glad to see you win."

"I do my singing for the Lord," he said. "Glad others enjoy it, me."

"I certainly did."

They fell silent just for a moment, but then, to Rhiannon's surprise, Trefor smiled. "You'll be owing me a congratulating kiss, then."

"What?"

He pointed upward. She looked, and there, directly over their heads, hung a bunch of the greenery she and Ceri had spread all through the house. She stared, unable to think of a thing to say.

Then Trefor took matters into his own hands. She didn't have to say a word. He placed a hand on her shoulder, curved a palm against her cheek, and pressed his lips against hers.

In that one brief, tender moment, Rhiannon felt all her girlhood dreams come true. The man she loved took the time to gift her with her first kiss.

Chapter 6

Every time she thought back to that first kiss, Rhiannon wanted to run and hide. Which is precisely what she did the moment Trefor pulled away.

How could she have behaved in such a silly, girlish way?

Even now, her cheeks burned at the memory of her cowardly response. Well, it wasn't her response to his kiss that had been cowardly. No, she'd enjoyed every second of that warm, tender caress.

The way she ran when Trefor whispered the most amazing words in her ear was cowardly.

"I've always loved you," he'd said.

She'd burst into tears and headed right for her bed. No amount of Ceri's cajoling had budged her. Mealtime came and went. Papa's request to join him also went unheeded. And Rhiannon did nothing but berate herself.

She'd been a fool to stay this long. She should have insisted Papa go with her to Cardiff for further medical care the moment his fever broke and he was able to travel. Now she faced a greater heartache than even she could have imagined.

Because now she knew. She knew what could be. If only. . .

But no. Nothing had changed. Trefor was still the superintendent of the mine. And she still felt the same abhorrent horror for the dangerous black hole. Who knew when it might unleash its murderous appetite again?

But now her fondest wishes were at arm's reach—for another woman perhaps. Another woman might be willing to risk the deadly possibilities in exchange for the joy of Trefor's love.

But how could she live if, after she shared in the beauty of that love, the lethal pit one day took her husband away? How could she face their children, should the Lord see fit to bless them that way?

She couldn't. Surely she'd go mad with the pain.

So she did the only thing she could. She began to pack her bags and prepared to make her escape as soon as Joseph saw fit to return.

Oh yes. That maddening man had done it again. He'd up and left one day. He'd murmured dire pronouncements of "emergencies" and "duties" and all sorts of other things. But they hadn't meant a thing to Rhiannon.

Nothing but yet another delay. Papa couldn't take on Joseph's duties in the office—whatever they might be—as well as the bit of his own work he'd started to do—at least, he'd insisted he couldn't. Rhiannon, her father had said, simply had to stay and help. There was far too much work for Trefor alone. He played on her pity, and although she felt quite certain he wasn't nearly as weak as he'd said, she had no way to prove her suspicion.

She wouldn't put it past Papa and Joseph to orchestrate the disappearance as just another way to throw her, again and again, in Trefor's path.

Which is precisely what happened one especially awful day.

"Rhiannon, dear," Papa said. "Please hand this to Trefor."

The three were in the office, a room she'd always thought of as huge. Now its walls felt far too tight around them for her comfort. She glared at the gleeful matchmaker.

"I'm sure Trefor can walk around and get it himself," she answered.

Trefor's jaw turned rock hard. "I'll be after making myself scarce, Miss Rhiannon."

"Nonsense, my boy!" Papa boomed his response with the overdone jolliness he'd adopted of late. "You're busy with those figures, and it's no trouble for Rhiannon to bring these sheets to you. Wouldn't want you to be losing track of your sums."

He stood. "I won't be forcing myself where I'm not wanted."

Something in his gaze shamed her. He'd been honest with his words of love. She, in turn, had been cowardly behind her silence—and hurtful with her evasiveness ever since.

She'd hurt the man she loved. She'd put her fears before his feelings, and this was the result. "Trefor. . ."

But he was gone.

And Papa wasn't pleased. "I hope you're satisfied," he said. "You've been more than rude to the most decent young man I know. And one who once was your dearest friend. I don't know what has happened to you, Rhiannon. Maybe Joseph was right after all. Maybe sending you to Cardiff did lead you to put on these airs and attitudes I don't admire."

Her father's words only served to make her guilt worse. But what could she say? That she loved Trefor but refused to let him know? That her fear mattered more to her than the feelings they shared? That she still felt she could never be the wife Trefor needed or he the husband she did?

No. It was better by far that Papa thought her haughty and mean. Someday she hoped she could change his mind, someday when the pain she felt now had eased to a dull ache, when she'd walked away from the love she'd dreamed of all her life.

"I'm sorry you see me like that." She left the room.

The time had come to leave for good.

But life had a way of turning her plans to nothing more than wishes. The next morning, as she sat down to a breakfast of toasted bread and tea, Joseph reappeared. But he didn't come alone.

"*Y Nadolig* is nearly here!" he exclaimed, his thin face wreathed in a wide smile. "I couldn't think of a happier way to celebrate Christmas than for the family to be complete."

He stepped aside. Uncle Owen and Auntie Deirdre, her arms stretched over her huge middle to hold baby Gwynneth close, walked in, wearing equally wide smiles. Meggie and Dafydd tumbled in behind them, their cries of greeting welcome and sweet.

Tears filled Rhiannon's eyes. "I've missed you!"

She slipped from the chair, dropped to her knees, and opened her arms wide. Meggie rushed into the hug and giggled, while Dafydd scrubbed the spot where Rhiannon smacked his cheek with a kiss.

"Ugh!" he said.

"You'll be changing that tune soon enough, my boy," Uncle Owen said. "Before you know it, you'll be looking for the mistletoe instead of letting chance catch you beneath a bunch."

Her uncle's words reminded Rhiannon of that other, more significant kiss. And the plans she'd so diligently made. Plans she could no longer carry out. Her relatives' presence in the family home made it impossible to return to theirs.

"Why—what made you come?" She turned to her aunt. "Isn't it dangerous to travel so close to your time?"

Auntie Deirdre smiled. "I don't feel any better or any worse whether I'm here or in my bed back home. So when Joseph came to deliver Mervyn's invitation, I couldn't resist. I wanted to be home by y Nadolig."

"But what if the baby comes too soon?"

"Then it comes," her aunt said. "I'm sure the Lord knows what He's about. He's been bringing babies into the world for much longer than I care to think."

An uneasy feeling started in Rhiannon's gut. "And how long do you plan to stay?"

Uncle Owen smiled yet again. "That is my surprise. I've closed the mill and given my people a holiday. We won't reopen until after Twelfth Night."

January twelfth! Rhiannon thought she'd go mad if she had to stay this close to Trefor for that long. But she couldn't let anyone know.

"I see," was all she said. When she thought she could speak without revealing her distress, she asked, "Does Papa know you're here?"

"Joseph says he's been expecting us and can't contain his anticipation," Uncle Owen said. "But we haven't been up to see him yet."

At his words, Joseph made a peculiar sound. Rhiannon slanted him a look and had to stifle a laugh. She'd be willing to venture a guess that Papa's unpredictable secretary had fabricated a tale of suggestion and hint worthy of Mr. Dickens for her relatives' sake. Papa likely knew nothing of the "invitation" Joseph had delivered.

"Ahem!" The secretary tugged on his lapels. "I'll be on my way to see if Mr. Mervyn is dressed and ready for guests."

Rhiannon chuckled. "Make sure you do *ready* him, Joseph. And do so with care. Shock so soon after his illnesses could be a dangerous thing."

She didn't specify to whom the shock might prove a danger.

Brown eyes narrowed and lips pressed down tightly. Joseph nodded then disappeared.

"That man!" she murmured.

"Oh dear," Auntie Deirdre said. "Do you think Joseph would do all this without Mervyn's knowledge?"

"I wouldn't put it past him." Rhiannon gestured toward the table. "Come on in. Join me. Mrs. Devane always has plenty of fresh bread, eggs—whatever you might want. And remind me to give Joseph a generous gift. I'm so happy to see all of you I'm about ready to give him a kiss."

"Lucky man, him," Trefor said from the door to the dining room.

Uncle Owen barked a laugh.

Dafydd repeated his earlier "Ugh!"

Rhiannon gasped, and her cheeks burned.

Meggie giggled and ran to Rhiannon's side.

Auntie Deirdre then cried, "Trefor Davies! Just look at how you've grown!"

"Thinking you have as well, Mrs. Wylie," he replied.

Deirdre patted her middle and laughed. "Can't be hiding it much longer, can I?"

His cheeks reddened, and Rhiannon knew she'd never seen a more appealing man.

"Not meaning that, me."

"But it's true," Owen said and held out a hand. "Owen Wylie, and Mr. Trefor Davies is. . . ?"

Trefor gave the hand a firm shake. "Mr. Gwynne's superintendent at the mine."

Owen's gray eyes flashed to Rhiannon and back. "I see. Good to meet you, I'm sure."

Trefor's jaw tightened, and he glanced at Rhiannon then gave a brief nod. "Having to head to the mine, me. A pleasure it's been."

He left.

Rhiannon's shame returned, but before she, too, could make her escape, her aunt caught her eye. "So that's how things are."

She shook her head, tears too close to the edge. "I don't know what you mean—"

"I'm sure that you do," Auntie Deirdre said. "But you'll tell me all when you're ready and not a minute before."

Her room offered a welcome escape. Rhiannon took refuge there and didn't come out until Ceri brought a message from her father. He wanted Rhiannon to join the rest of the family around his bed.

She donned her cheeriest smile and opened the door. "Here I am," she said. "What did you—"

The rumble of a train cut off her words. Then the ground shook as it rolled along the tracks. Rhiannon froze.

No train ran at that time of day.

Ceri's wail rose up from the kitchen. Doors opened and slammed shut. The chapel bells rang out a wild alarm.

Her father leaped from the bed, yanked on the thick wool robe draped over the foot of the bed, and rummaged for his sturdy work boots. "The mine!" he cried without any need.

They all knew what the sound meant.

Rhiannon heard the echo of an earlier rumble, felt the earth's quake of years ago; she saw the grief on her mother's face and the wooden caskets holding her grandfather's and uncle's remains.

Her temples pounded with her pulse.

Pain squeezed her heart.

Her breath failed.

Nausea rose.

But it wasn't what she saw, heard, remembered, or felt that kept her immobile and chilled. It was the last words Trefor had uttered that scared her the most.

"Having to head to the mine, me."

She began to shake. At first, shudders ran through her. Then her hands shook. Her knees felt weak, she went lightheaded, and her teeth chattered. Had it not been for the gentle hand that reached out and clasped her elbow, Rhiannon would have fallen to the floor.

"He's more than the mine superintendent, isn't he?" Auntie Deirdre asked.

Rhiannon couldn't answer. She felt herself led, and when something firm caught her behind her thighs, she sat. The tears began to fall, and only then did she realize her aunt had guided her to Papa's bed.

For long, silent moments—silent in the room, since outside the chapel bells continued to sound their alarm—she cried, fear ruling her every thought, hampering her every breath. And then the bells, too, fell silent.

Rhiannon realized the room had emptied but for her and Auntie Deirdre. "Where did they all go?"

"Mrs. Devane took the little ones. Joseph asked her when he, Owen, and Mervyn left for the mine."

Rhiannon moaned. "That soulless pit—"

"It may be soulless, but you aren't, and neither am I." She reached out her hand. "Let's pray."

Her first impulse was to refuse her aunt, but then, from the deepest corner of Rhiannon's mind, the image of Trefor singing at the eisteddfod gained strength. As did the contrast between his faith and hers—or rather, her lack of faith.

Because she now knew that her fear was nothing more than a lack of faith. She'd prayed for greater faith, for the Lord's help there. But now this happened. Would what faith she had be enough? Would the Lord hear the prayers of a woman like her? Did she have strong enough faith?

Rhiannon didn't know. The one thing she knew was that her faith felt strong enough to try.

She reached out, took her aunt's hand, and bowed her head in prayer.

Chapter 7

Soon, however, prayer wasn't enough. Rhiannon felt the gnawing need to go to the colliery and see the devastation herself. True, whatever accident had taken place had done so deep beneath the surface of the earth. But the real devastation took place in the lives of those left to pick up the pieces aboveground.

What a terrible cloud to mar the joy of the upcoming Christmas...

She hurried to her room, rummaged through one of her two packed valises for a heavy wool cape with a hood, threw it on, and then ran outside. On the way to the pithead, she noticed other women and children, quiet and frightened, exiting cottages and hurrying down the road.

The frigid wind bit at her face and seeped under the edges of her cape. She pulled the heavy fabric closer but knew nothing would take away the cold she felt deep in her heart. A prayer for Trefor bubbled up to her lips. She prayed he hadn't been inside, that all the men had already left before the explosion or cave-in, but she feared her hope was in vain. It was too early in the afternoon for all work to have ended before the explosion, and somehow she knew that Trefor was inside that shaft.

She started to run but found it hard to stay upright. Patches of dirty snow hid slick ice. Her smooth shoes weren't adequate to negotiate the frigid, winter-rough surface.

What had gone wrong? Many times she'd sat in while Papa and Trefor discussed all the safety improvements they'd made, all those they planned to implement. She knew how careful they were with each and every aspect of the mine, the equipment, and especially the lives of the workers. It seemed to her they thought through every precaution and implemented it as soon as feasible.

She hurried past the chapel, sparing no more than a glance for the two elderly deacons who stood in the doorway, deep frowns on their brows. She approached the mine, her steps slowing the closer she came to the cluster of sheds. A large group had gathered outside the wooden structure that covered the entrance. Whispered conversations sped back and forth, the sound almost as sharp as the rush of the bitter wind.

Rhiannon spotted a familiar figure to the left of the slag pile, filthy with dirt and coal dust. "Papa!"

Everyone turned. She'd cried out her dismay, while no one else dared speak out loud. Still, she couldn't believe her father had gone inside the killer pit.

She hurried to his side. "Why did you—"

"Go home, child," he said. "This is no place for you."

"Are the men inside? How many? Was it an explosion? Or did a roof cave in? What happened?"

"Rhiannon, please. Go home." He wiped a shaking hand down his worried face. "We don't know much yet. Yes, there are men inside, but we don't know how many, much less what actually happened. Let us do our work, and you'll know as soon as we do."

When he wouldn't meet her gaze, she knew. "He's in there, isn't he?"

Papa's shoulders sagged. In a shaky voice, he said, "Trefor went in after his men. I tried to stop him, but he wouldn't be held back. After a bit, I couldn't continue.

All that time I spent in bed has weakened me more than I thought."

The regret in his face hit her hard, but not as hard as the truth. "They're not coming out, are they?"

A woman not two feet away gasped then glared. She turned on Rhiannon, a hand raised as if to strike her. Papa caught the woman, who crumpled in his arms and sobbed.

Over the head of the terrified woman—a miner's wife—he met his daughter's gaze.

"Go home," he repeated.

This time she obeyed. As though she wore a sign proclaiming her a foul thing, those who'd gathered to wait parted, unwilling to risk even a brush with her skirts. The whispers resumed, this time angry and hot, turned against her.

Tears blurred Rhiannon's vision, but despite the sudden blindness, she knew what she had to do. She couldn't bear it; the man she loved would surely die in the ruined shaft. She could not—would not—stay until they brought out his body, crushed and broken, from the murderous hole in the earth.

Rhiannon gathered the fullness of her gown in her hands and ran home. There, she gave thanks for the foresight that had kept her from unpacking her bags. She called Joseph, who, unhappy but ever the respectful retainer, helped her drag her luggage to the carriage house.

There, he fell on his knees, shrouded by the shadows inside. She'd never witnessed her father's secretary's prayers, but she was doing so now. She noticed the tears in his eyes.

He glanced up when she called his name.

"I have to leave," she said. "Now." She gestured toward the door. "My bags are out there. Please, *please* help me go. Hitch the horses for me. I'll have one of the station hands return the carriage once I catch the train."

"Where will you go?"

"To Cardiff. I'm sure Mrs. Llewellyn, Auntie Deirdre's housekeeper, will let me in. I just—just can't stay here. I don't belong. I never should have come back."

"Nonsense!" he said, his voice reminiscent of Papa's at his best. "Your father needed you. He was ill and you helped him. Surely you know how much he loves you. He needs you here. You mustn't leave."

"You don't understand. The colliery"—she spit out

the foul word—"is everything here. And I can't bear even the thought of it anymore. It's a killer; it respects nothing and no one, and I can't watch it kill—"

"Mr. Trefor."

The floodgates opened, and while she'd cried on her way back from the mine, that had been nothing compared to the grief and misery that racked her now.

"He's down there. He went after his men. . . ."

Joseph closed his eyes. A wince of pain shot through his face. "I'm so sorry, miss."

"So am I." She took a deep breath. "Surely you must see now that I have to go. Please don't try to stop me. The train's due in about a half hour, and I intend to leave on it."

"I can't change your mind, can I?" he asked in a tired voice.

"No."

"At least let me drive you there. You're too overwrought to handle Mr. Mervyn's lively pair, and the roads are covered with snow and ice."

She shrugged. As long as she reached the station in time to catch that train to Cardiff, what did it matter who held the reins?

Moments later, her bags secured, they took off, and

Rhiannon turned for a last look at the village that had both given her life and taken her love. Now that she was leaving again, she would never return.

Rhiannon lost herself in her memories—thoughts of her childhood, those happy days before her grandfather and uncle died, before Mama died, too. She thought of the many times she'd followed Trefor, how she'd dogged his footsteps, wanting to be near him at all times.

His friends had teased him; he'd defended her. True, he'd only seen her as an irritating pest, but his kindness toward her had never failed. Trefor had always been warmhearted, generous, honorable, decent, and true. And those qualities were the ones that made him follow his men that day.

Yes, she loved him, but she didn't have the courage to stay. She didn't want to see his dead body. And even if he survived, she doubted he'd come out whole. Many of the village's residents had lost limbs inside that mine. She didn't have the courage to see him maimed.

She asked the Lord's forgiveness for her weakness, for her cowardice, for her secret departure. She hadn't even left a note to explain herself. She'd only thought to go, to put as much distance between herself and the mine as she possibly could.

The carriage gave a sudden lurch to the right. "Whoa!" her father's secretary-cum-driver yelled.

"Joseph?" she called. "Are the horses. . . ?"

"Everything's fine, Miss Rhiannon."

The vehicle continued to clatter over the rough surface. She bounced on the hard seat. "Are you sure?"

"Not to worry. One of the carriage wheels must have hit some ice."

One of the horses gave a sharp neigh then, and the carriage took another lurch. Joseph muttered just low enough for her not to catch what he'd said. Then, louder, he added, "Just sit back, miss. We'll be at the station any minute now—"

This time, the carriage went left while the horses went right. A hideous shriek rent the air. The vehicle heaved and shuddered over to its side. Too fast for her to react, Rhiannon's world tumbled away. Top and bottom traded places; she flew through the air; her arms and legs hit the seat, the floor; finally, something struck her head.

Everything went black.

Trefor prayed as he and two of his men dug through the rubble that blocked the passage through to the newest part of the mine. "Besides Rhys Morgan," he said as he drove his shovel deep again, its metal edge scraping against stone and dirt, "any other men missing?"

"Two," Lloyd Maddox said. "Ewan Kimball and Dylan Keith."

He prayed for the men, that his and Lloyd's efforts achieved results before Ewan, Dylan, and Rhys died from the gas—*if* they hadn't already died from injuries in the initial collapse.

They dug for hours, through thick mud and rock. They sweated; rocks scratched and scraped them; they bruised knees, foreheads, elbows, and ribs. Determination carried them forward, their lamp a symbol of the hope they carried in their hearts.

Through every second of toil, the memory of Rhiannon's fears played in Trefor's mind. He hadn't been inside the shaft at the time of the accident, but he knew too well how often rescuers were trapped by subsequent collapses. He'd told Rhiannon he trusted God, and he did. He had to each time he entered the mine.

But Trefor knew, in a corner of his heart, that he also valued the knowledge of his skill and strength. He prided himself in his ability to work the mine and survive. That, and the ease with which he could lead the men safely through completion of a day's work.

Had he been prideful? Had he called it faith when his successful toil deep within the ground had been a matter of self-centered pride?

He and Lloyd had heard a number of frightening creaks since they'd reached the blockage of fallen rock, broken wood, and as always, the ever-present mud. The wooden supports for the mine roof over their heads might not hold up; in fact, they probably wouldn't hold up much longer. If the initial collapse had weakened other areas and something tested them again, he and Lloyd could end up just as trapped as the other men.

Had Rhiannon's fears of the mine been more realistic than his simple faith? Would today's accident claim three—five—lives? Would he ever see Rhiannon again?

Unwilling to give in to fear, clinging to faith in his Lord, and determined to save his men, Trefor persevered. He worked through the exhaustion in his every bone, through the damp coolness of the earth, through the pain in his ragged hands.

When he thought he couldn't go on for one more inch, another loud creak rang out overhead. But instead of retreat, the threat served only to strengthen his faith.

If it were the Lord's will, all five of them would get out alive. He wouldn't doubt the Lord.

Seconds later, he broke through the blocking mess. On the other side, three injured but still-breathing men met him with gratitude in their eyes.

"Thank you, Father," he breathed.

And the roof cried out again. Everything around them shook. Rhys Morgan waved toward his two bleeding companions. "Crawling I'll be," he said. "Help them, or we'll all be dying in here."

"It's lost we'll be without You, Father," Trefor cried. "Help us now!"

Inch by miserable inch, the three men worked to ease the way out for the two more injured miners. Then the worst came to pass. To their rear, over the spot where they'd just been, the roof crashed down again.

Their lamp fell and went out. Rocks flew down around them. The earth bucked and rolled. Dust surrounded them and fouled their air. But Trefor refused to doubt his God, the God who'd brought him to the trapped men in time.

"Just a bit farther we're needing to go, Lord!"

He didn't know how exactly they did it, but an eternity later, Trefor spotted the flicker of a far-off lamp.

"Help!" he cried. "It's help we're needing now. They're still alive."

And help they had. A flurry of activity relieved him and Lloyd of their precious burdens. Hands reached out to support even them. Blankets swathed them. Crystal-clear water soothed their parched throats. The praises of the villagers rose toward heaven.

Trefor wept. "Thank You, Father."

If he were never to have Rhiannon's love, at least he now knew that this was where he belonged. His sinful pride would have no more place in his life. He knew that by the grace of God, and only by that grace, he had reached his men. The Lord hadn't abandoned him in his moment of need; Trefor had placed his faith right where it belonged when he'd trusted the almighty Father. That faith would see him through even the heartbreak he knew was to come.

After a new mine accident, there'd be no question about Rhiannon's feelings. She'd only be leaving the village sooner, if she hadn't already left.

"Lord?" Joseph asked as he tried to hurry over the icy road. "This wasn't how it was supposed to come out.

Why? Why did it have to end this way?"

But no answer was forthcoming this time.

And he couldn't stop to wait for the answer that would come. Rhiannon had been hurt when the horses spooked, fled, and the carriage overturned.

He regretted his stick-thin build. Were he a larger, stronger man, Joseph felt certain he would have been able to carry Rhiannon to safety. As it was, he had to hurry back to the village to fetch help.

It didn't help that he'd twisted his ankle in the accident.

Tears had filled his eyes when he saw the gash on Rhiannon's forehead. She hadn't responded to his many pleas, even though he could see she still breathed. Unable to help her himself, he'd protected her from the wind and made her comfortable with the robes and blankets in the carriage, then began the hobble back home.

Who would help them, he didn't know. With that dreadful accident at the mine, everyone in the village was sure to be at the pithead, waiting for any news.

"Don't abandon me now, Lord! I know I'm not utterly blameless here, but for Rhiannon's sake, lead me to help."

As soon as he saw his men in caring hands, Trefor knew he still had one more thing to do. "Coming back I'll be," he told Mervyn. "This won't be taking long."

The Lord's blessed mercy toward the miners gave Trefor the strength to hurry to the Gwynne home. He wanted Rhiannon to see him, dirty, scraped, and bruised but still alive. She had to see that mine accidents weren't always fatal, that the Lord had seen and would continue to see him through.

He pounded on the heavy wooden door.

Mrs. Devane answered. "Who'd be knocking down our door—Mr. Davies!"

His breath came out in a ragged burst. "Rhiannon! Where is she?"

The plump lady gave him a look of distress. She wrung her hands and shook her head. "Gone. Wanting to play with her, the children were, but when we went to her room, we found all her things gone."

If he hadn't leaned against the doorframe, Trefor feared he would have dropped to the ground like one of those chunks of stone in the mine.

"Too late, I am," he said in a rough voice. Although

he knew the answer, he had to ask. "Will she be back soon?"

Mrs. Devane shrugged. "I couldn't be saying. I didn't see her, and I haven't seen a note, a letter—nothing."

Despair filled him—but not for long. The clock in the Gwynnes' entry vestibule clanged out five chimes. He realized that, while he'd thought days if not weeks had passed as he dug his way through the mine debris, it had been only a few brief hours. There was a chance he could reach the five-fifteen train before it left. That is, if she'd planned to return to Cardiff on that train.

"Returning to Cardiff, is she?"

Again, Mrs. Devane shook her head. "I wouldn't be knowing, Mr. Davies. I didn't see her. . ."

He didn't wait for her to finish her response. He hurried down, again avoiding the ice and snow that had turned the road into a treacherous mess. If Rhiannon hadn't yet left, Trefor meant to see her one more time.

"Father? Giving me one more miracle, would You be, please?"

Head down against the bitter wind, Trefor hurried the short way down the road to young Dr. Gruffud's home. He knew the man would be there, tending to the injured miners, since that was where he kept his medical supplies. Trefor had made sure Lloyd understood that the men needed the physician's expert care, that they had to be transported to the doctor's place.

Old Dr. Gruffud answered the door. His rheumatism had bent him double, but the man's eyes remained as sharp as they'd ever been.

"How would I be helping you?" he asked in his gravelly voice.

"Your horse!" Trefor said. "Could I be borrowing it for a while?"

Seconds passed as the elderly doctor studied Trefor. Something in his expression, or perhaps it was just the filth and blood on his face, must have led him to respond to the urgency in Trefor's plea.

"Go on. But don't be bringing him back all sweated and leaving him to dry all night."

"I would never do that, and I'll be thanking you proper when I return."

Moments later, Trefor guided the gentle animal down the road, cautious to lead the beast's steps away from the patches of ice. With every pace, he breathed another prayer, a chain of pleas for Rhiannon's understanding, for her willingness to believe, to trust the Lord, even in this other matter between them.

Trefor meant to press her, to make her admit her feelings for him. Somehow he knew her fear for his life had made her flee. And her fear wouldn't have been so sharp had she not felt for him as he felt for her.

He hoped.

"Trefor!"

The weak voice sounded familiar. He looked down and, to his shock, saw Joseph on the roadside, cold, disheveled, his steps uneven and unsteady.

"What's happened?" he asked as he made to dismount.

"No!" the secretary cried. "Don't stop. Miss Rhiannon is hurt up ahead. The horses slid on the ice—we were on our way to catch the train. Hurry! She must not be out in the cold any longer. She's been there too long already as it is."

Before Joseph had finished his disjointed explanation, Trefor had urged Dr. Gruffud's horse back up to his previous pace. This time, however, hope spurred his ride.

Moments later, he reached the overturned carriage. He found Rhiannon, chilled, pale, weak, and unconscious but still alive. He'd never seen a lovelier sight. With infinite tenderness, he gathered up in his arms the woman he loved, the one he believed God meant for him to wed. With Rhiannon's head pressed against his heart, he led the horse toward the village.

When he reached Joseph, the canny secretary took advantage of Trefor's reluctance to release the injured woman, clambered onto the steed, and led them all the way back.

As they reached Dr. Gruffud's home, Rhiannon's eyelids fluttered open for a second or so. He didn't think she'd registered much, not even that he held her in such an intimate, compromising embrace. She sighed then breathed a word.

His heart took flight on the wings of that breath.

"Trefor," she said.

Epilogue

In the following days, Rhiannon recovered her health, and her cheeks once again glowed with the soft color of summer roses. Trefor had left her side only to visit his injured men. He hadn't dared stay away any longer than that; he had to make sure she didn't try to bolt again.

"You must be trusting me some."

He smiled. The local lilt had returned to her speech, something she'd obviously worked to lose while in Cardiff. But what she asked of him was no laughing matter.

He shrugged. "And how should I be doing that? While I went after my men, escaping you were. How can I be trusting you again?"

"Should I remind you what you said before?" When he sent her a questioning look, she continued, "It's not me you should be trusting, but rather God. You said you trusted Him to bring you out of that shaft collapse. You want me to trust, but you should be trusting Him to show me how to live with that fear."

He arched a brow. "Seeing that truth, are you now?"

Rhiannon, lovely in a pale green dress that played up the shade of her eyes and the red lights in her hair, made a helpless gesture with her slender hand. "I'll never trust the mine, Trefor. Lying I'd be if I said otherwise. But you did come out alive."

"At this time of year," he said, "surely you'll be seeing how God sent us His Son to set us free. That freedom isn't only from the fear of falling mine walls. Trapping you, that fear is."

"It's not that easy, Trefor. I'm trying—"

"Trying alone. The Father will be giving you the strength to break the bond of fear—if you let Him. Keeping us apart, that fear is, too."

Rhiannon reached out and touched his hand. The warmth of her gentle caress reached deep into Trefor's heart. Before he could react, she spoke.

"I asked the Father for more faith, and His answer

was the mine collapse. I don't know how I can trust."

"Trusting Him, I am when I go into the mine, and look!" He gestured to himself. "He's brought me out in one piece all the time."

"But—"

"But you ran in fear. And far away from the collapsed mineshaft is where you were hurt."

"Oh, but that wasn't much. Not like what happens in mine collapses."

"Yes. More could happen in the mine. But breaking a neck in a carriage accident is no small thing. Caring for you, the Father was, too. Just like He cared for us in the mine, for me."

Her eyes opened a bit wider. "He did, didn't He? Protected us both."

"Of course, and He'll be doing it always. For the life He's given us."

She thought a moment. "I do know His love is constant and certain. I don't see how else we both would have come through mostly unhurt."

She ran a finger over a knuckle that still bore a scrape from digging through the fallen rock. Then she laced her fingers around his. Trefor felt the need to hold her in his arms, to bring her close, but he didn't dare.

They'd come so far, and he didn't want to scare her off again.

In a quiet voice, she asked, "A gift from Him, this is, no?"

He squeezed her hand but didn't respond.

She continued. "Away from Him, we're lost, in the dark, a dark as deep as that mine of yours. But with the Lord's help, we can come through—no, He can bring us through."

Trefor sent up a quick prayer and took the chance. He slipped an arm around her shoulders. Rhiannon didn't pull away, but rather leaned closer to him.

He pressed a kiss onto her temple. "Wanting faith, you were. Sounds like the Father showed you the way to that faith. Drawing you closer to Him, He is."

Her green eyes glowed with so much love that his heart took flight. "He's drawing me closer to you, too."

"Thanking Him, I am," he said in a voice that shook just a bit. "I'd be saying, too, His lost lamb has now been found."

"And staying where He's brought me, right here at your side."

And stay she did.

Days later, in the deepest, darkest hours of Christmas

Day, just before the sun began its rise, the singing of
hymns and carols during the traditional *Plygain* service
finally drew to a close. That's when Rhiannon and
Trefor made public their troth and announced to the
village their intention to wed.

The sun rose and brought light to the village. The
chapel bells rang to celebrate the birth of Christ. And
in heaven, angels rejoiced that another lost lamb was led
back to the fold of faith.

Welsh Rarebit

4 slices whole-wheat bread, toasted
4 slices Canadian-style bacon, warmed
4 slices ripe tomato
1½ cups shredded sharp cheddar cheese
¾ cup whole milk
½ teaspoon of mustard powder
1 teaspoon Worcestershire sauce
Dash ground red pepper
1 beaten egg

Place a slice of toast on each of four plates. Top each with Canadian-style bacon and a tomato slice. Set aside. For cheese sauce, in a heavy saucepan stir together the cheese, milk, mustard, Worcestershire sauce, and red pepper. Cook over low heat, stirring constantly, until cheese melts. Slowly stir about half the hot cheese sauce into beaten egg; return mix to the saucepan. Cook and stir over low heat until cheese sauce is thick and bubbly.

To serve, spoon sauce over toast. Makes 4 servings.

GINNY AIKEN

Ginny, a former newspaper reporter, lives in Pennsylvania with her engineer husband and their three younger sons—their oldest son married and flew the coop. Born in Havana, Cuba, raised in Valencia and Caracas, Venezuela, she discovered books early and wrote her first novel at age fifteen while she trained with the Ballet de Caracas, later known as the Venezuelan National Ballet. She burned that tome when she turned a "mature" sixteen. Stints as a reporter, a paralegal, a choreographer, a language teacher, and even a retail salesperson followed. Her life as a wife, a mother of four boys, and the herder of their numerous and assorted friends, brought her back to books and writing in search of her sanity. She's now the author of twenty-five published works, a frequent speaker at Christian women's and writer's workshops, but Ginny has yet to catch up with that elusive sanity.

Colleen of Erin

by Tamela Hancock Murray

Jesus said unto him, If thou wilt be perfect,
go and sell that thou hast, and give to the poor,
and thou shalt have treasure in heaven:
and come and follow me.

MATTHEW 19:21

Chapter 1

Dublin, 1820

Finn Donohue stood behind the counter of his store, filling out an order for more horse blankets. Cold weather had brought about a demand that had almost depleted his supply. Finn never wanted to turn away a customer for lack of merchandise. His aim was for Donohue's Mercantile to be known for stocking the largest variety of quality goods in Dublin. His formula so far had proven successful.

The front door bell tinkled, signaling that one of the last customers of the day had arrived. Finn shivered as a burst of cold air blew in before the door shut. He spun around on his heel. Just as quickly, warmth filled him as he watched Colleen Sullivan approach the counter in a graceful stride. His heart skipped a beat. Colleen was the prettiest girl in all of Dublin, what with her hair as black as coal and her eyes as green as the emerald grass of his beloved Erin.

Finn noticed that she had made sure the heavy wooden door closed behind her. No doubt she valued the heat from the store's potbellied stove. Seeing such caution pleased him on a cold December day. Though a small gesture, it proved that the wealthy Sullivans knew the value of a farthing.

As soon as her glance caught his, he greeted her. "Top o' the evening to you, Miss Sullivan." Finn tipped an imaginary hat in her direction and let his lips form his most engaging smile.

"Top o' the evening to you indeed, Mr. Donohue." Her eyes danced above cheeks that were as rosy as spring cherries no matter what the season. Her speech, while still conveying a soft Irish brogue, possessed a refined polish cultivated during her Swiss finishing school years. "I'm glad to find you are still open. I was afraid I might have been too late."

"Aye, you are out a bit late today. But even if you had knocked on the door at the stroke of closing time, I would have kept the store open for you." Like Colleen, Finn owed his precise speech to travel abroad. Unlike Colleen, he didn't come from a wealthy family. His *máthair* had sacrificed to provide the means and knowledge to lift him up to the merchant class, and he wasn't about to forget her dedication to him.

Colleen smiled. "Thank you for your kindness, Mr. Donohue, but I would never impose upon you to keep the store open for me, especially since my own carelessness caused my delay. I was setting out my supplies for tomorrow's mending, only to discover I had run out of white thread."

"Well, we can't have that now, can we? Let me fetch a nice big spool for you."

She smiled and brought the sun with her.

As Finn moved toward the rack that housed the spools of thread, he heard her add, "Oh, and after that, I'd like my usual order of candy."

He turned and grinned at her. "For the orphans, eh?"

"Of course. And I'm hoping the doll for Kathleen's birthday will be arriving soon from London."

"Any day now, Miss Sullivan."

Colleen stared at the toy display, but Finn discerned that her concentration wasn't on his current offerings. Instead, her countenance radiated wistfulness. "Oh, I do so hope Kathleen likes the doll I chose for her."

"Why, I'm sure she will. What little girl wouldn't love a doll with auburn hair and a green velvet dress? But if the one you chose doesn't meet your expectations, you may certainly choose another one. I ordered several in anticipation of Christmas."

"Then many little girls in Dublin will be happy on Christmas morn. But I'm sure I'll be very pleased."

He set the spool of white thread on the counter for her approval.

She inspected the thread and then nodded.

"Little Kathleen should be grateful for anything she might get, if you ask me," he commented. "Without you and your generosity, those orphans would have lean birthdays. No birthday presents at all, I would conjecture. You are kind to remember each one."

"The Lord has blessed me beyond what I deserve. It is my duty and obligation to share with those less fortunate. A duty and obligation I fulfill with great joy." She broke out into a genuine smile.

" 'God loveth a cheerful giver,' " Finn quoted from

scripture. "Considering how much you give again and again to His glory, I'd say that you can rest assured He loves you."

"And He loves you, too."

"But I am not nearly as compassionate as you. You're softhearted, Miss Sullivan. No wonder you're well thought of by us mere mortals in Dublin. And not just by the orphans."

A slight blush colored her cheeks.

Finn decided to change the subject to minimize her embarrassment. "Oh, I have something I'd like to show you. You mentioned that you'd like to give a set of pearl earrings to your máthair. I took the liberty of ordering a pair. See if you like them." After withdrawing a key from his pocket, he unlocked a drawer under the counter where he kept special treasures. A little purse containing a dainty pair of pearl earrings awaited. He opened the purse and presented the earrings to Colleen. "I hope they please you, Miss Sullivan."

She gasped when she viewed the small but nearly perfect pearls. "I am delighted, and my máthair will be, as well. She always likes to say that a buckle is a great addition to an old shoe."

Finn and Colleen shared a laugh. The emotion

made him feel good, and he wondered what it would be like to share mirth with Colleen all the time. Seeing her admire the pearls, he allowed himself the briefest fantasy of giving her an emerald pendant one day. Such a stone would match the color of her eyes.

Colleen pulled the string on the purse to secure the pearls. "Thank you, Mr. Donohue. Please add these to my bill. I'll settle with you at the first of the month, as always."

"I know you will. If only my other customers were as faithful as you. There's no excuse for not paying a bill, I always say."

"But sometimes there is a good reason," Colleen pointed out. "Hard times and unexpected circumstances can occur to the best of us."

"I suppose a few bad debts are inevitable, but I have little patience with those who can do better. Forgetting a debt doesn't mean it's paid." He made a mental note to add Colleen's amount to his ledger and noticed her eyes had taken on a distressed light. "I'm sorry. I have no business bothering a pretty lass with the problems of business. I'd much rather pass the time of day speaking of pleasant matters." He regarded Colleen's purchase. "I hope you don't mind me for complimenting you on your taste. In fact, I'm giving my own máthair a string of pearls to mark the occasion. You inspired me, if I may say so."

Her face softened. "You may say so. Oh, speaking of Máthair, that reminds me. She's baking today, and so I need four cinnamon sticks if you have them."

"Indeed I do. Of the finest quality." He hadn't meant for the pride to show in his voice, but it had. He wondered how many other nearby merchants could boast as much. He reached into a spice box and withdrew the number requested. Their sweetly pungent aroma pleased him.

Colleen inhaled delicately as she watched him pack the spices. "Ah, that cinnamon smells delightful."

"I was just thinking the same."

She lifted her dainty forefinger. "Oh, and one other thing. Has the silk I ordered arrived yet?"

He pursed his lips. "Not yet, I'm sorry to say. Next week, I hope."

A flicker of disappointment visited her pretty features before she composed herself. "That is quite all right. Nothing you can do to change that. I won't engage the seamstress until I have the fabric in my own hands."

"That is a wise practice." Still, he hated that he

couldn't make the order arrive a moment sooner than it would. "What I can change is how quickly the silk gets to you once it arrives at the store. When it does, I'll deliver it to your house myself. In person."

"You will? Oh, don't let me trouble you so."

" 'Twould be no trouble at all, Miss Sullivan. Your farm is only a few miles out of my way. I enjoy the excuse for a drive in the fresh air. I find it invigorating."

"I hope that's not just blarney you're speaking to me, Mr. Donohue. But delivering the silk yourself would be mighty kind of you."

He smiled, pleased that he could help. "And how else may I be of assistance to you on this fine day?"

"I believe that will be all. My order is never a large one. 'If you buy what you don't need, you might have to sell what you do.'"

"A wise proverb," Finn agreed. " 'A heavy purse makes a light heart.'"

His own reference to money reminded him that plenty of work needed to be done and he hadn't heard any movement from his worker as of late. He swept his gaze over the store, looking for his employee. Finn wasn't known to be lenient, expecting from his assistants more than an honest day's work for an honest day's wages.

His gaze captured Darby, who was once again staring out the window instead of going about his chores. The idea that the boy wasted time on the job vexed Finn to no end. "Darby!"

The young man lurched out of his daydream. "Yes, sir!"

"You're getting a late start. Lose an hour in the morning and you'll be looking for it all day. I need you to make sure we are fully stocked on fabric. You know Mrs. O'Malley bought several yards to make clothes aplenty for her brood yesterday. I wouldn't want to miss a sale because we can't lay our hands on the appropriate broadcloth."

Darby nodded.

"And then be quick about the sweeping. Indoors and out."

"Yes, sir. I will." Darby nodded in several quick motions and hurried toward a table overburdened with fabric.

"Mr. Donohue, he looks like he's scared to death of you!" Colleen chastised him, although in a voice too low in volume for Darby to hear.

Finn felt a tinge of embarrassment, but not enough for him to give any ground. "You know me, Miss Sullivan.

I have little patience for ne'er-do-wells. Darby would rather spend the day chasing leprechauns than working."

Colleen looked at Darby and shook her head. "He's but a boy."

"Then he should learn sooner rather than later that poverty waits at the gates of idleness." Finn looked in his employee's direction and tried not to sneer. "That lazy boy will be finding himself out of work if he doesn't mend his ways."

"Have you no compassion?" Colleen's eyes darkened.

"I have compassion for those who work, I do." Finn clenched his fist around the pencil he was using to record Colleen's purchases. Slothful men reminded him too much of his *fáthair*, who'd abandoned his máthair when Finn was an infant to pursue idle dreams. That was almost three decades ago. Finn had never seen his own fáthair.

"You'll never hear me speak ill of the laborer," Colleen conceded, reluctance coloring her tone.

"I am a firm believer in working hard, as you know. Through work, I am determined to give my máthair the life she deserves. The life my fáthair denied her." Though he had always loved Colleen, moments such as this reminded him why he had never asked to court her. Resisting the urge to wag the pencil at the young woman, he settled for tapping it upon the counter. "You, Miss Sullivan, could learn a lesson or two from me. To wit, why you keep that no-good overseer on your farm, I'll never know."

She stiffened and lifted her chin ever so slightly. "Ross O'Hara may not toil with the diligence you think he should, but he needs the job and I'll keep him on at my place as long as he's willing to stay."

Finn observed Darby picking up the broom and gave himself a mental pat on the back for getting through to the boy. "See how Darby is working now? One need not be harsh to encourage employees to work. And he knows he'll be getting his pick of gifts from the store to give his family this Christmas, courtesy of me. But I'm not as gullible as you are, Miss Sullivan. Ross O'Hara is taking advantage of your soft heart, he is."

Colleen huffed. "Might I ask you to tend to your own affairs." She grabbed her order from the counter and tilted her head at him once. "Good day, Mr. Donohue."

Alarmed by her upset tone of voice, Finn snapped his attention back to Colleen. "Miss Sullivan, allow me to help you get those goods to your carriage."

She lifted her nose. "Good day, Mr. Donohue."

With those words, she left. He thought of pursuing her, but another patron passed Colleen on her way through the door.

Finn turned brief attention to Joey. The well-dressed man, wearing a fine walking suit, was one of his best customers. If he could multiply Joey tenfold, Finn would be the richest man in Dublin. Deliberately putting aside his frustration in allowing Colleen to see him in a poor light, Finn cleared his irked expression and replaced it with one of an eager merchant.

"Good evening, Joey. You're just in time. I was almost ready to call it a day." Though he addressed his customer, Finn's gaze remained on the door through which Miss Sullivan had exited. Watching her pass by the front window, Finn wished he could have nailed his lips shut. Why did he have to let down his guard and irritate her?

He exhaled. Colleen Sullivan would never understand why Ross O'Hara vexed him so.

She didn't know that Finn loved her.

As Joey browsed, Finn mused to himself. How could he expect Colleen Sullivan, a woman born of privilege, to understand how he had come up from nothing? Not only had his máthair toiled, but Barney O'Conner had taken an interest in him. When Mr. O'Conner offered young Finn a job as a shipping clerk for his importing business, Finn didn't hesitate to take the opportunity. For seven years, Finn labored and learned the business, going abroad, thanks to his máthair's largesse, money she earned by scrubbing floors in Dublin's fine homes.

Later, when the mercantile came up for sale, Mr. O'Conner helped Finn purchase the business. For the past nine years, Finn had built his customer base to where he turned a fine profit and had long since paid back Mr. O'Conner, with interest. The rewards had been long and slow in coming.

Only in recent times had Finn felt he made a living good enough that he could consider taking a wife. Colleen Sullivan was his first choice. An image of her loveliness floated into his consciousness, making him smile.

"Do you have the cinnamon sticks I ordered, Mr. Donohue?" Joey asked, interrupting his thoughts.

Finn took his gaze from the window. Colleen had passed long ago, anyway. "What's that?"

"The cinnamon," Joey repeated without the least bit of vexation. "I ordered cinnamon sticks last week."

"Oh. Those. Yes, I have a few. I just sold four to Miss

Sullivan. I hope her request won't disfurnish you."

"I'm sure it won't. I only need three."

Finn counted what remained in his supply. "I have more than three. And superb cinnamon it is, too."

"I have no doubt about that." Joey paused. "And the other spices?"

Finn searched his brain and recalled that the previous week, Joey had requested pepper and licorice. "Not yet, I'm afraid. My spice merchant has proven unreliable as of late. The situation has gotten so dire that I'm thinking of taking my business elsewhere."

"Oh, don't make such a decision on my account. I can wait."

"You are generous as always, Joey."

He shrugged. "And why shouldn't I be? I've been blessed."

Finn nodded, remembering how Colleen had uttered almost the identical phrase moments before.

"I see behind you the bolt of linen I ordered. A mighty fine shade of purple it is, too. I can always depend on you for quality wares."

Such a compliment delighted Finn. "Pleasing the customer has always been my aim."

"If you could provide me with a few other items, I

would be pleased. First, two pairs of silk stockings. And some bay rum scent. Then I'd like to see the fragrance on display—the one in the opaque bottle." Joey nodded toward costly floral perfume and, after inspection, agreed to take it without expressing concern about its price.

Finn remembered another item his customer might like, since he was in the habit of buying expensive gifts for a woman. Finn wondered if Joey purchased such lovelies for his wife, sweetheart, or máthair. He had hinted that he'd be pleased to be privy to such information, but Joey was never forthcoming about the woman in his life. Still, Finn could make some reasonable deductions. "I received some fine silk fans this morning. I put aside a lace one I thought you might especially like for your—wife?"

"Yes, I would like to take a look at the fans."

As usual, Joey made the purchase without offering any clues. Instead of asking for credit, he paid his bill in full. For such promptness, Finn was grateful. He hated to extend credit but knew such a practice was a necessity if he hoped to stay in business.

He bade Joey good day as curiosity struck, and not for the first time. Who exactly was Joey? Why didn't he ever tell Finn his last name? Did he live in Dublin or out in the country? Perhaps seeing the man's convey-ance would offer him a clue. "I know that bolt of cloth is heavy. Might I help you take your goods to your car-riage, Joey?"

"No, thank you. Your offer is quite generous, but I assure you, I can take care of myself."

Finn lifted his finger, hoping to stop him. "But—"

"I shall see you early next week, in hopes that those spices have arrived." With that, he made a quick exit.

"That's the second instance in less than an hour," Finn muttered. In spite of himself, he ran after his cus-tomer. For the first time, he wished he hadn't attached a bell to the door of his establishment. He hated that the clanging sound would alert Joey he was being followed.

Finn stuck his head out and looked left, then right. Since winter was deep, night threatened. He saw not a single being in the twilight. He wanted to take a chance and, after choosing a direction, run after the elusive customer. Yet he couldn't. No use in having everyone in Dublin think him daft.

Chapter 2

Holding her shopping basket, with her free hand, Colleen pulled her redingote trimmed in ermine more closely to herself to ward off the cold. She rushed to her awaiting carriage at the side of the store. She couldn't get out of Finn Donohue's sight soon enough. The man exasperated her. All she had wanted was to go into his store and procure a few goods to last her through the week and perhaps engage in pleasantries with the proprietor. Why did he insist on upsetting her with his meddling? She wondered if she deserved to be vexed for not allowing her driver to accompany her on her errand, wanting to see Finn without being under her driver's watchful eye.

Yet gladness joined vexation. She thought back to how her steps felt lighter, her heart merrier, in Finn's presence. How handsome he was! As if it weren't enough that he possessed a fine abundance of wavy black hair, a pleasing complexion, and eyes as blue as the sea—no, that wasn't all. He had told her she inspired him! She sighed. He had kissed the Blarney stone, that one had.

Then she recalled how he had criticized her compassion, calling her gullible. Gullible!

Too exasperated by the remembrance to be gracious, she ignored the driver's offer to assist her in boarding the carriage. Stomping up the step, she let out a sigh and thrust her goods toward the side of the carriage, not caring in what position her reed basket landed on the black leather seat.

Colleen plopped down with more force than needed, sending her garments flying. The driver gave her a curious look and opened his mouth slightly as though he planned to ask what had put her in such a mood. She shot him a glance dark enough to discourage questions, before he shrugged and shut the door.

As she smoothed her skirt with gloved hands, she thought about Mr. Donohue. Everyone, including her máthair, thought Colleen to be the perfect match for the merchant. The cherished daughter of a deceased gentleman farmer and his wife, Colleen was denied nothing by her doting máthair.

That fact evidenced itself in her style of dress, sewn according to the latest pattern from Paris. Her decorative bonnet was fresh and elegant, and her redingote reflected a military style beloved by the French at the time. The garment boasted many buttons and cords and, in Colleen's case, ermine trim at the hem, collar, and cuffs. Underneath such a fine coat, her pelisse was equally fashionable, sewn of richly dyed cotton and featuring a high waist.

Mrs. Sullivan had suggested more than once that a merchant would appreciate—yea, even benefit from—such a fashionable wife. Known to be a fine dresser, Colleen possessed the attire and superb confidence to wear clothing well. Such a reputation would attract more business for Finn should they wed. Surely, Mrs. Sullivan suggested, the ladies in town wanted to look as elegant as Colleen, and they would be certain to buy expensive cloth and fine lace from the store in an effort to emulate her mode of dress. Aware of the luxuries Sullivan money afforded, Colleen could see such logic. Yet she wanted to marry for love, romantic that she was.

So why did she love such an uncompassionate ox?

The question remained unanswered as the carriage passed the milliner's shop she patronized regularly, a druggist she hardly ever saw thanks to robust health, and two pubs she had never entered. All the storefronts, including Finn's, had been whitewashed in anticipation of the celebration of Christ's birth. She spotted a couple of acquaintances and sent them a friendly wave. Her family farm was located just outside the city, so soon they had passed the outskirts of town and were clip-clopping up the lane to the farmhouse. Visions of Finn rolled through her head. If only she felt free to give him her most ardent affections. Could he love her, too? But it was no use.

Lord in heaven, why did Thee give me feelings for a man with so little mercy for others? Or am I being disobedient to want to be near him? I am ready for Thine answer, whatever it may be. In Jesus' precious name, amen.

Moments later, after Colleen disembarked and made a special effort to show the driver courtesy to amend for her previous rudeness, she entered the farmhouse she had always called home. The dwelling, whitewashed, as were the stores, looked fresh and ready for Christmas. She smiled, heartened to see such a vivid reminder of the Babe's purity.

Though Colleen never considered the house impos-
ing, it was larger than most in the area, with several
ample rooms. The structure had been solidly built by
Colleen's ancestors.

Anticipating Colleen's arrival, Mrs. Sullivan greeted
her at the door. "Did you get that thread you were
after?"

"Yes, I did, and the other things on your list, too."
Colleen kissed her máthair on the cheek as was her cus-
tom whenever she returned from a journey, no matter
how long or short. Remembering the pearls, she slipped
them in her pocket so her máthair wouldn't spy them.

Mrs. Sullivan took the basket and gave the goods
a quick inspection. "Good. I see he even had the cinnamon. Now we can bake our Christmas cakes for the
church dinner and make some wassail on Christmas
Eve, too."

"Aye." Colleen braced herself for the next question
she knew to be inevitable.

"And how was Mr. Donohue?" Lively emerald eyes,
identical to Colleen's, took on a light of mischief.

"He was well." Colleen didn't look at her máthair
but concentrated overly on removing her bonnet and

redingote with the help of a maid.

"Waited on you himself, did he?"

Colleen nodded. "As always."

A look of satisfaction crossed Mrs. Sullivan's features. "You know, if you play your cards right, I believe he could be yours."

"Máthair, you know how I feel about that. Why, he was after that boy in his store—Darby, I think his name is—to sweep the floor as it was. He'd work me to death."

"Afraid of a little labor, are you?"

"Nay. But Finn's a hard man. Complaining about those who aren't able to pay their bills on time." Colleen didn't hold back a grimace.

"You must remember that you've never had to worry about money, but Mr. Donohue has not been so fortunate. A merchant must collect on his debts, or he won't be in business long. Try to see things from his point of view."

"I suppose you're right," Colleen admitted. "It's just that I'd like to see him demonstrate a wee bit more compassion for his fellow man."

"He might come around one day. You never know," Mrs. Sullivan said. "So did you see anyone else of our acquaintance?"

"Mrs. Kelly was shopping with her daughters, and Mr. Fitzgerald sends his regards. And I passed Joey on my way out of Mr. Donohue's store."

"Joey. Did he have anything to say beyond a greeting?"

"Nay. He is a mysterious one," Colleen conceded. "Funny, no one ever mentions seeing him except at the store. Not at church, not about town, just at the store."

"Oh, I'm sure people have seen him here and about. We just don't know about it, that's all." Mrs. Sullivan smiled. "Maybe he wants to be secretive, rich as he is. I understand he keeps the Donohues in fine style with his purchases."

"Surely Finn is grateful."

"No doubt. He told me again today how he wants his dear old máthair to have a better life than he had—a life she earned many times over. She worked so hard to make the money to send him abroad so he could learn his trade and make contacts with importers."

The older woman's eyes darkened, and she flitted her hand as if dismissing a fly. "That fáthair of his was no good."

"Máthair!"

" 'Tis true. But enough of that. I know it isn't right

to gossip. Besides, it's almost time for dinner. And Cook has made my favorite—mutton stew."

The following day, Colleen knocked on the door of one of the city's orphanages, Mallory House. Ian Mallory, an orphan who grew to be wealthy, had bequeathed his ancestral home upon his death to the benefit of the city's parentless children. Colleen enjoyed her visits to Mallory House. The number of children never grew past twenty, so she could learn each child's name and disposition.

"There ye are, Miss Sullivan. 'Tis good to see ye once again," the gray-haired mistress, Miss O'Leary, greeted Colleen. "The children are waitin'. Yer visits are the highlight of their week, they are." She stepped aside for Colleen to enter.

"And they are a highlight of mine," Colleen assured.

"Miss Sullivan is here!" she heard little Dylan say.

His announcement brought forth a tidal wave of children. They shouted greetings, their voices echoing in the foyer.

"Now, mind yer manners!" Miss O'Leary cautioned.

Colleen laughed. "I don't object to a little noise all

in fun. But I must say, if you are all good during story time, there will be a piece of candy for each one of you. Special from Donohue's Mercantile."

Whoops and hollers echoed.

"I'm not sure ye'll be able to calm them now that ye've made such a promise," Miss O'Leary warned, a teasing light dancing in her blue eyes.

Still laughing, Colleen withdrew a book from her satchel, saying a silent prayer of praise for the children and their joy. As the hours waned, her thoughts turned to Finn. What would he think of spending an afternoon with the orphans? Surely he could find compassion for such tenderhearted little souls, their plight no fault of their own.

Or could he?

"Back again, I see." Finn smiled at Colleen the following day when she returned to the store. "You must be anxious about that fabric."

In spite of herself, she felt her heart lighten. This time she had allowed her driver to accompany her into the store, so she knew he would be listening even while pretending to be otherwise occupied. She made sure her voice sounded nonchalant. "Yes, after my last visit to the orphanage, I realized more than ever how much in need they are of fresh clothing. I hope to fashion a simple shirt for each of the children. They will enjoy something new."

"They are sure to welcome such efforts."

Colleen looked yearningly at the toy display. "No doubt they'd each like a toy, too." She looked Finn straight in the eyes. "You know, Mr. Finnigan is donating a crate of oranges so each child might have a fresh piece of fruit on such a special day."

Finn let out a low whistle. "Oranges, eh? The grocery business must be fine for Finnigan to go to such extravagance."

She chose an apt proverb as a response. " 'Keep your shop and your shop will keep you.' "

"Aye, the proverb cannot be bettered," Finn conceded. "Finnigan is doing a good thing. A nice orange will help keep the orphans healthy."

Once again, Colleen made a point of eyeing a stock of toys lined along shelves on the far wall. A selection of dolls with painted china heads, wearing colorful dresses and matching bonnets, sat side by side, their eyes of black lacquer seeming to beg for a little girl's love.

Wooden pull toys, shaped like ducks, dogs, and cats, were painted in vibrant colors. Colleen visualized the children playing with any number of games Finn had on display, and running with the balls. She cast her gaze toward him and caught his conflicted expression.

Finn crossed his arms and leaned against the counter. "I know what you're going to say next, Miss Sullivan. You're wanting me to donate some toys, aren't you?"

"Well, now that you say so, it would be lovely for each child to receive not one but two gifts each." Colleen glanced at the top of the counter and back. "I'm supposing that would be a nice thing for you to do."

"But I was hoping to sell those toys." His voice sounded plaintive.

"Of course you were. But surely you have time to order more to replenish your stock before Christmas, eh?"

He shifted his weight from one leg to the other. "How many would you be needing?"

"Oh, not many," she replied, stalling for time as she went down her mental list. "Eighteen?"

"Eighteen!" He swallowed and adjusted his collar.

"That's not such a large lot. If the orphanage were full, I'd be asking for twenty."

"Twenty! In that case, eighteen doesn't sound so

great a number." He let out a labored sigh and glanced at the dolls, wagons, pull toys, balls, and wooden hoops. "Oh, all right. I believe I can find it in my heart to let the children have a few toys."

She exhaled an unrestrained gasp. "Oh, Finn—I mean, Mr. Donohue—that's very kind of you. Very kind indeed."

"Well, as you say, when the Lord has blessed a man, he can give back a few farthings."

Suddenly she felt led to pursue the thought that had occurred to her earlier. "Won't you help me take the toys to the children? It will mean much to them—and to you, to see who'll be benefiting from your generosity."

"Really? You want me to accompany you?"

Regret seized her. Perhaps she had been too bold. "Well, I—"

"Why, certainly. I can do that. Now that you mention it, I wouldn't mind seeing the little ones myself."

"Tomorrow, then?" Her tone of voice sounded too eager to her ears.

"I can do that. Now go on and choose the toys you want."

"That would be delightful." Regarding the selection of wares, Colleen revisited her own childhood. Choosing a toy for each child, be it a new doll or hoop for a girl or a wooden pull toy or ball for a boy, pleased her. After a few moments, she had completed her joyful task. "Thank you, Mr. Donohue."

A moment later, Colleen didn't bother to suppress her smile of victory as she left the store. Maybe there was hope for Finn Donohue after all.

Chapter 3

As soon as he told Colleen he'd take toys to the orphans, Finn regretted the promise. He liked children, at least the idea of children, but the thought of entertaining them made him feel like the goose sent with a message to the fox's den.

He didn't know much about children of any age or description. He realized—not for the first time—how odd he and Colleen both were as only children in a country full of large families. Brothers and sisters could have helped him. As it was, he felt lost. Had his fáthair stayed, Finn no doubt would have enjoyed the companionship of many siblings. Another reason to resent him.

He remembered the apostle Paul's admonition in

Colossians 3:8: "But now ye also put off all these; anger, wrath, malice, blasphemy, filthy communication out of your mouth."

The last ones on the list troubled him little. Anger at his fáthair, well, that was another matter.

"To put off repentance is dangerous," he muttered under his breath.

"Sir?" Darby asked. "Did ye say somethin'?"

Startled, Finn looked over at the boy and noticed that, for once, he held a broom in his hand. "Just muttering to myself. Go on about your business."

"Yes, sir."

Resolving to be more careful with his musings, Finn decided to put together a few orders for delivery. The task, though not thoroughly engaging, took his mind off his fears.

Concentrate on Colleen.

Colleen! His admiration and fondness—even love— grew with each encounter. He took in a breath at the thought of her beauty, her kindness, her soft voice, her confidence. . . . Colleen possessed every attribute he wanted in a woman, and more. But could he fit in her world? He had to show her he could.

But how? Finn didn't want to make a fool of himself.

The only way he thought he might avoid that was to let Colleen do all the talking the next day. Maybe then he could survive the afternoon at the orphanage.

Colleen heard hoofbeats slow from a trot to a stop and wheels rolling, then braking, against the dirt path leading to the farmhouse.

Finn!

She set aside her embroidery and rose from her chair to peer out the window.

"Sounds like your beau is here," Mrs. Sullivan called from the kitchen.

"Máthair! He's not my beau!"

Mrs. Sullivan approached her, wearing a wide grin. "Maybe one day he'll be asking to court you."

Colleen let out an exasperated groan that she hoped would conceal her feelings for her visitor. All the time she'd been engaged in household tasks, images of Finn stayed close at heart. "Máthair, please. I'm not looking for a suitor."

"If not, then you'd better be thinking of it." The older woman inspected her daughter. "You are lovely now, with an abundant head of hair and smooth cheeks. And with such a slim figure, you wear your clothes well. If I may say so, you remind me of myself at your age. But remember, you won't be young and beautiful forever. One day you'll look like me, with gray in your hair and wrinkles around your eyes."

"Oh, but you are still beautiful," Colleen protested.

"To a daughter, maybe. But as to marriage, well, don't delay forever. I'm wanting grandchildren. If your fáthair were still alive, God rest his soul, he'd be saying the same." She tapped Colleen on the shoulder in a cautionary but kind gesture.

"I know, I know. But I don't want to marry any man who doesn't understand my compassion for others."

"Give him time. If I know you, Colleen Sullivan, you'll have him seeing the light faster than a rabbit running from a wolf."

"I may try," Colleen admitted, "but the waiting man thinks the time long."

A knock on the door hushed the women. Mrs. Sullivan, still spry, rushed to answer. "Mr. Donohue!" she greeted as though she hadn't seen him in a decade. "So good to have you here."

Charmed, Colleen exchanged greetings with Finn. Her delight waned as she shifted her concentration from her máthair to the man before her. She hadn't expected him to be dressed in a crisp morning suit. True, she had chosen to don a flattering pink frock trimmed in white fur, but Finn looked smarter than she'd ever seen him. She wondered if the orphans would think him a visiting dignitary instead of a merchant. Still, he looked too handsome to deserve any admonishment.

"Come on in and have a cup of tea," Mrs. Sullivan offered.

"Aye, if only I could spare the time. But the orphans await." He smiled at her máthair in a way she had seen him look at his best patrons.

The stars in Mrs. Sullivan's green eyes showed Colleen that the older woman was captivated. "You'll have to be sure to stop in for a good long visit and some tea with us next time. Cook made some fresh bread, too, and we have plenty of clover honey. Maybe you can partake with us when you bring Colleen back later today."

"For you, Mrs. Sullivan, I will make the time."

"I'll wager you wouldn't close the store for me, though," she teased.

He rubbed his clean-shaven chin and looked up at the sky as though he were in deep contemplation. "I don't know. I might have to think on that proposition awhile."

Colleen's máthair laughed, giving rise to an unwelcome flash of jealousy. *What am I thinking? 'Tis my own máthair, and Finn must soften his heart before I could even think of him as a husband for me. Oh, what is wrong with me? What gives me the idea he'd even consider me? Pride has reared its ugly head. Lord, please stop such uncomely emotions in my heart!*

"Mr. Donohue, we'd best be going, or the mistress of Mallory House will wonder what became of us," Colleen managed to say.

"To be sure," Finn agreed. "We wouldn't want to disappoint her—or the little ones."

The ride to the orphanage wasn't long. For the first time, Colleen wished miles rose between them and Mallory House. She found that she enjoyed sitting beside the storekeeper. His fine countenance turned more than one woman's head as their carriage passed. Perhaps part of their curiosity resulted from wonderment as to why she rode with Finn. Yet Colleen had the distinct feeling that the women were admiring his comeliness—and might have been feeling a wee bit of envy. Though she and Finn didn't touch, she sat closely enough to enjoy his nearby warmth and the manly scent of his spicy shaving lotion, whereas they could only peer from a distance.

As she expected, Finn didn't say much along the way. Colleen, not wanting to bore him with mindless chatter, restrained herself to remarks on the weather and a few mutual acquaintances from church they spotted. Otherwise, she enjoyed the companionable silence. She had a feeling that he did, as well, although she also sensed a nervous spark. She wondered why.

Before long, their carriage approached Mallory House. The home looked like a large, uncomplicated box. Like other houses in the area, it had been whitewashed for Christmas. Shutters of dark wood made a splendid contrast with the light hue.

"There they are!" called one of the orphans, Sean, running across the lawn as their carriage approached.

Two other boys, Joseph and Patrick, ran toward them, calling out greetings as Colleen and Finn disembarked. From the corner of her eye, Colleen observed Finn, monitoring his response. The boys looked clean, but their clothing had been mended several times. At least Miss O'Leary kept them all in shoes during the winter.

"Miss Sullivan, did you bring us Christmas toys? I heard that's what you were plannin' to do." Patrick tugged on the sleeve of her redingote.

"Hey, that's not polite," Joseph admonished with a poke to the little boy's ribs. "Miss O'Leary would take to ye with the wooden spoon if she heard you say that."

Patrick flinched. "Sorry." His eyes grew wide, and he drew closer to Colleen. In a whisper he asked, "Well, did ye?"

Colleen laughed. "I cannot tell."

"She did! She did!" Patrick bounced up and down, red curls flying.

Finn's hearty laughter filled the air. "Word gets around here fast, I see."

"Yes, sir. No fella can keep a secret around here, at least not for long. Too many ears around," Sean informed him.

"Say, mister, who are you?" Patrick asked. "Are you one of them big London soli—solipticures?"

"Do you mean 'solicitors'?" Colleen guessed.

Patrick nodded. "Aye, that's it. Are you one of those? The last time one of them came by, Mary and Agnes left."

"Nay, he's the storekeeper, you dunce," Joseph said. "Don't ye know anything?"

"He's not old enough to go to the store. You know

that." Sean shoved Joseph gently enough for a reprimand, but not enough to strike him off balance.

"You didn't come to adopt one of us, did you?" Patrick persisted.

"No, I'm afraid not." Colleen felt compassion tug at her heart. If she could adopt the entire lot of orphans, she would. But she could make their lives in the institution easier, so she did as she felt the Lord leading her.

Colleen noticed that Sean held a ball she had given him for his last birthday. "Were you getting ready to play a game, boys?"

She saw Finn eyeing the ball. "Boys, I haven't played a game of football since I was but a lad. What say you to a game after I help Miss Sullivan unload—I mean, after Miss Sullivan and I visit with Miss O'Leary?"

"Aye!" Patrick exclaimed.

"Aw, he just don't want to do his chores," Joseph said.

"Chores await, eh?" Finn answered. "Well then, let's put off our game. Work always comes first."

"It can wait," Sean said.

"Unwillingness always finds an excuse," Finn countered. "I wouldn't want to get you in trouble with the mistress. We can play another time."

"Oh no, Mr. Donohue." Colleen pulled him aside and spoke in a voice that couldn't be overheard. "It's quite all right. Miss O'Leary would be happy to let them play for a time. You go along. There isn't that much for me to do. I'll tend to our errand."

Finn looked back at the carriage. "I can't allow a lady to fend for herself. What say I deliver the goods to Miss O'Leary? Then the boys and I can play while you read to the girls; after I help them with one of their chores, that is. Miss O'Leary may think it's fine to delay work for company, but never let it be said that I encouraged sloth. Laziness is a heavy burden."

"Oh, I'm sure they would be delighted for you to help before they play." Colleen observed his suit. "You're not quite dressed for work, I must say."

He regarded his attire. "Never mind. I'll choose a chore that's not so messy."

"Well then, that's a splendid idea. I'll send out the other boys to take part in the game."

"Other boys?"

"Of course. You didn't think this was all of them, did you?" Colleen jested.

"Oh. I—I suppose not."

She thought she spied a frightened look on his face.

Why was he afraid?

If the boys noted Finn's unease, they didn't let their expressions show it.

Joseph didn't miss a beat. "They should be finished with school soon. We're out because our lessons are done!" He beamed.

Finn laughed. "The schoolhouse bell sounds bitter in youth and sweet in old age."

"School will never seem sweet to me," Sean said.

"Me, either," Joseph concurred.

Colleen chuckled. "I'm glad to see you boys agree on something." With that, she left Finn with his new friends.

Later, after Colleen had visited with the girls, reading to them and assisting with their candlewick projects, Colleen bade them farewell and ventured to the front lawn. Seeing Finn having such a good time running back and forth, she held back, hating to interrupt. He looked like such a little boy himself, playing as though years had melted. After Finn scored, he looked up and seemed surprised to see Colleen standing near. He sent her a victorious look then rushed to her.

"Are you finished with the girls already?" His cheeks were ruddy with winter air and exertion, and his breath looked like steam when he exhaled.

"I'm afraid so. You can come back and visit another time. I know the boys would love to see you again," Colleen said.

Patrick joined them. "Do we have to stop?"

"Well, let's see now." Finn consulted his pocket watch. "I'm afraid we must. I didn't realize the time had flown so quickly. I hope the girls don't feel neglected that I didn't stop in to say hello to them, as well."

"Aw, who needs a stinkin' ol' girl?" Patrick asked.

The adults laughed, and after Finn bade farewell to the boys, he escorted Colleen to the carriage.

"Your gifts pleased Miss O'Leary," Colleen said. "And they pleased me, too. I hope now that you've visited the orphanage you aren't sorry you made the donation."

Finn smiled. "I'll never regret anything I can do for the orphanage. Those boys touched my heart. I hope you don't think me less of a man for saying so."

"Oh no!" She placed her hand on his sleeve but didn't let it linger too long. "I think you more of a man for admitting you can have—can I say—compassion for others."

Had she just uttered such a thing about Finn Donohue?

He grinned. "Didn't think I was capable, eh?"

She felt her face blush hot. Could he read her thoughts? Then again, Finn's outpouring of kindness had extended to the boys only upon her suggestion, and so far, just for an afternoon. Surely a life of hardheartedness would be more difficult to change than what could be accomplished in so short a time.

Meanwhile, her own heart throbbed with pain. She wanted Finn to learn compassion not to please her but to make his life better. She prayed that being with the boys was only the beginning of Finn's yearning to look beyond himself and his hurts and extend kindness to others.

Having mused enough, Colleen responded, "Oh, I think you always have been capable of compassion. Then again, who couldn't feel sorry for those poor children, parentless as they are with no place in the world to go but Mallory House? I thank the Lord every day that Miss O'Leary is kind to them."

"Yes, and they are there through no fault of their own," Finn pointed out. "Surely they deserve a little joy on Christmas morn."

"Yes, they do." She realized they had reached her house. "Here we are. I hope you will accept Máthair's invitation to dine with us."

"I'm not so sure she offered me a meal," Finn pointed out.

"Maybe she didn't. But I am."

Mrs. Sullivan greeted them at the door, surrounded by the aroma of the muttonchops and parsnips that would be the evening's meal.

"Finn accepted my invitation to dine with us," Colleen told her.

"Good." Her jolly smile confirmed that she was pleased.

Though Finn was pleasant to Mrs. Sullivan during dinner, Colleen noticed that his gaze stayed on her most of the time. She didn't feel uncomfortable. Instead, she found she wanted this man—a man she thought she had known all these many years—to remain near her.

Mrs. Sullivan excused herself to package a plate of leftovers for Finn's máthair. Colleen's heart beat faster when she realized they were alone in the parlor.

He shifted his weight from side to side and spoke in a shy tone she didn't recognize from the usually confident storekeeper. "I—I had a fine time today, Miss Sullivan."

"As did I. The boys certainly took to you. That pleases me very much." She paused, working up the nerve to ask him something she'd been contemplating. Courage gathered, she looked him in the eye. "I have a request. Please call me Colleen."

His face brightened. "I may?"

Suddenly feeling shy and hoping she wasn't making a mistake, Colleen glanced at her shoes and then returned her gaze to his face. She nodded.

"Colleen." He sighed. "How sweet your name sounds on my lips."

"Yes, it does. Say it again."

"Colleen." He smiled. "Say my name. My Christian name."

"Finn." Just uttering his name aloud brought joy to her heart. A heart she still had to protect, lest she lose it forever.

Chapter 4

After bidding Colleen farewell, Finn whistled as he all but skipped across the Sullivans' lawn. Fresh with joy from being granted such a privilege—the privilege of calling Colleen by her Christian name—he was in an exhilarating mood. He leaped into his carriage and urged the horses homeward. Could Colleen ever love him enough for him to ask her hand in marriage one day? The looks she sent his way hinted that she could, yet something about the way she carried herself told him that the time to declare his love to her wasn't right. Not yet. One day, maybe. Hopefully that day would be soon.

Daydreaming of the present and future with Colleen,

Finn wondered why the horses came to an abrupt stop without his say-so.

Then he saw it—a fluffy white form in the path.

The sheep bleated.

"A sheep! What's that sheep doing out and about?" He jumped from his conveyance and headed toward the stray animal. "How did you get out, boy?" A bleat from another sheep caught Finn's attention. It, too, had escaped and wandered down the path. Finn noticed two more not far off. "What is the meaning of this?" he asked no one in particular.

He picked up the sheep and surveyed the part of the fence that shielded the Sullivan farm from the path. Soon he discovered his answer. A gap in the wooden fence had proven too much for the sheep to resist. Several had escaped from the pen, and Finn had no doubt the entire flock would be headed for freedom before all was said and done. Colleen's overseer, Ross, would need to summon the dogs to gather them back up and repair the fence in haste. In the meantime, Finn returned to the pen the one sheep he had rescued himself before he hurried back to the house to let them know what had happened.

Colleen greeted him. "What are you doing back so

soon? Is something wrong?"

"I'm afraid so. Your sheep are escaping from the pen as we speak."

Colleen gasped. "Oh no! Did Ross leave the gate open again?"

"He leaves the gate open? Why, such carelessness is inexcusable for a farmhand, much less an overseer."

An embarrassed look covered her face. "I know. But I'm afraid he does take spells of carelessness from time to time."

Anger reared its head in Finn's heart. How could Ross be so uncaring about the property he had been charged to protect? Thinking there was no time to debate the issue, Finn decided to get right to the point. "The gate isn't the problem. I found a gap in the fence."

A flicker of disgust—something Finn had never seen cross Colleen's face—appeared before she composed herself. "I mentioned that to him when I saw it earlier today. I thought he would have mended it right away, as I asked. He knows the sheep will get out if there's a break in the fencing."

Finn tightened his hands into fists, though he kept them at his sides. "That man ought to be throttled."

"Let us not condemn him."

Finn appealed to fact and reason, as much to keep himself calm as to convince Colleen. "I know his reputation. He loves the bottle more than his work."

"He means well."

"So you say. You'll never plow a field by turning it over in your mind," Finn pointed out. "Surely after this, you'll consider firing him."

"My farm help is none of your concern, Finn Donohue." Her strong voice brooked no debate. "Let me concentrate on the task at hand."

He wanted to argue that he was concerned about the woman he loved, but her expression remained steely. Chastened, Finn's guilt spurred him to help Colleen summon the dogs to gather the stray sheep.

"The first thing we need to do is find Ross." Finn tried to keep disgust out of his voice. "Where is that worthless farm manager when he's needed?"

"I'm not sure where he might be at present." The edge had returned to Colleen's voice.

Finn withheld further comment. "Since we're not sure, why don't I take to fixing the break for you? No point in gathering up all the sheep if we just put them right back in the pen with a torn fence." Finn's motive wasn't pure. A tough chore would give him the chance to spend some of his ire in a productive way and keep himself in Colleen's good graces, too.

"Making that repair would be kind, but are you sure you have time?" She looked at him, concern and admiration in her eyes. "And what about your suit?"

He didn't flinch. "A suit is only raiment. And for you, Colleen, I have all the time in the world."

She blushed and looked down at her skirt as though it had become interesting. He wasn't sure if her response was good or bad.

He cleared his throat. "Have you got a hammer and a few spare pegs in the shed I can use?"

"As far as I know, yes. Look on the top shelf in the back."

He nodded and set about his errand.

Inside the shed, he found more than tools. Not expecting to see anything living except perhaps a dog or cat, he jumped back to see a lump on the floor underneath a brown horse blanket.

The lump snored.

Moving closer, Finn knelt beside the form and moved the blanket away from the source of the snoring. The face revealed belonged to Ross O'Hara. The man clutched an empty tankard, keeping it near his lips even as he slumbered.

Finn shook him by the shoulder. "Ross O'Hara!"

The balding man, who looked older than his fifty years, stirred and groaned.

"Wake up, Ross! What are you doing asleep back here, and with a cup at that? Have you been drinking?"

Eyes fluttering open, he came alive. "Finn Donohue? What are ye doin' 'ere?"

Finn stood to his feet and looked down at the idle man. "I had dinner with the Sullivans. But never mind that. Why are you sleeping instead of doing your work?"

"The workday's long over, that's why. And what business is it of yers?"

"It's my business when you don't mend the fence."

"The fence?" A twinge of remembrance crossed his craggy features, but he recovered by taking the offensive. "This ain't yer farm. It's the Sullivans'. I do as they say, not as you wish."

"If only. Miss Sullivan just told me she asked you to repair the fence. Why didn't you?"

"I'll get to it tomorrow." Ross settled back in as though he planned to return to slumber.

Finn knelt down far enough to slap Ross on the

shoulder. "You'll get to it, all right. But tomorrow is too late. The sheep are already out."

"Huh? What sheep?"

How could he ask such a ridiculous question? Finn stood erect. He folded his arms in a conscious effort to hold back his temper. "The sheep you were supposed to be tending. Those sheep."

Surprise lit Ross's dulled eyes, and he sat upright. "They got out? I didn't mean for that to happen."

"Sure you didn't. Now get up and help us get them back into the pen. If you can."

Ross tried to stand but wobbled.

"I'd tell you to fix the fence, but you're in no condition. You should have done your job before you took to the bottle. Better yet, you should have done your job and left the bottle alone."

"I–I'm sorry. I'll look around and see if I can find some of the sheep. How many's missin'?"

"We're not sure yet. Where are the other hands? Can't they help us in the search?"

"No, I let 'em all off."

"All of them? What were you thinking?"

"I didn't mean to. They asked one by one for this reason and that, and before I knew it, I'd told them all they could have the day off, and the night, too. They've all gone into town for some fun, I imagine."

"You'll have to look for the sheep alone, then. Maybe this will be a lesson to you," Finn couldn't resist adding.

"I'll do me best."

Finn wanted to retort that he wasn't sure that Ross's best was good enough, but Finn had already vexed Colleen as it was. With rancor, he gathered the hammer and pegs and made his way to the fence. Though repairs weren't his profession and he wasn't donned in work clothes, he completed the chore quickly. As he predicted, the exertion released some of his anger toward the drunken farm manager. Even better, he felt good when he rose to his feet and eyed his handiwork, knowing he had done a good deed for Colleen.

As he admired his achievement, Colleen and the dogs approached. A few sheep followed in turn.

Finn counted five sheep. "Is that all of them?"

"I'm still missing four," Colleen said.

"That's four too many. Let's keep looking."

Ross approached from the woods. "Three. Ye're missin' three."

Finn noticed that no sheep accompanied the farmhand. "It's already back with the flock?"

Ross shook his head and stared at the ground. "Wolves got him."

"Wolves! Oh no!" Colleen groaned. "What a horrible death. The suffering that sheep must have felt. The poor animal."

"That's a misfortune, sure enough, but there's no use in standing around moaning and crying," Finn said. "Let's hurry and see if we can find the others."

An hour later, Ross, who had sobered thanks to embarrassment and forced exercise, gave up the search. Finn concurred.

"I'm sorry, Mr. Donohue," he said, breaking the silence on the long walk back to the farm.

"Don't go telling me you're sorry. Tell that to Miss Sullivan. And if I were you, I'd be ready to pack my bags. I know you'd be out on the street if you were working at my store. You wouldn't have lasted a day."

Ross sneered. "I believe it. Ye're not known for mercy, Mr. Donohue."

"I dispense mercy to those who deserve it." Finn remembered the orphans and ignored Ross's disdain.

Back at the house, Colleen awaited their return. She greeted them at the back door, an anxious look on her face. "Were you able to find the sheep?"

The men shook their heads.

"Oh, those poor animals."

"Those poor animals have lost you some income," Finn pointed out. "All because of this lazy farmhand. If he had done his job, none of the sheep would have gone astray."

Colleen looked at Ross. "You are dismissed for the evening. I'll see you tomorrow morning." Instead of sounding a reprimand, her voice was weary.

Ross slumped and nodded, then turned to go back to his quarters.

"Dismissed only for the evening?" Watching Ross depart annoyed Finn all the more. He tightened his lips so hard he could feel the blood rush. "Don't be afraid. Fire him if you like, Colleen. I warned him on the way back from the search that he could expect to lose his position over his negligence."

Colleen stiffened. "I have no doubt you'd fire him if you were me, but you are not. I thought I told you that I have my reasons for keeping him in my employ."

"I'd like to know what those reasons are."

She crossed her arms, the motion matching her lips twisted in vexation. "All right, since you were kind enough to fix my fence and look for my sheep, I suppose

I owe you that much. Ross is a distant cousin. We keep him here because his penchant for drink keeps him unemployable by strangers."

"I can testify to that. I found him asleep, clutching an empty cup, and his breath reeked of ale."

She slumped. "Usually the farmhands under his supervision realize his weakness and try to do what they can to make up for Ross's inconsistencies. I don't know what happened this time. He seems to be getting more and more careless. So you see why no one else but family would hire him."

"So you say. But why should you even put up with such laziness? Family or not, he should be of some use if he's being paid." Finn felt rage boil up to his neck. "You can't allow yourself to take in every stray. You cannot save the world."

"I know. The Lord has already saved the world."

Her answer, delivered with the serenity of an angel, irked him all the more. "I know that, Colleen. But being a good Christian doesn't mean you should allow everyone to take advantage of you." Seeing her chin drop, Finn decided he'd better leave before he said something he might regret. "I'm sorry. Perhaps I should not be so free with my opinion. I only want what's best for you."

"And I believe, in your way, you do. But for now, I must bid you a good evening."

Colleen's words sounded frosty, and her expression looked nothing as it had earlier when she'd granted him leave to call her by her Christian name. Finn's heart, so warm before, felt petrified. He wanted to protest, but Colleen shut the door. Gently. Yet firmly.

Chapter 5

The next day, Finn could hardly concentrate on work. Every time the bell at the store rang, he looked up, hoping Colleen might have decided to stop by. Noon came and went, and no Colleen.

His thoughts ran wild. Maybe she was avoiding him on purpose. Maybe she could never love him. Maybe she was even thinking of asking him to return to calling her "Miss Sullivan." Maybe he had been too harsh on Ross.

So many regrets and speculations. If only he could turn back the clock!

He thought of Darby. As instructed, the boy was taking account of the pickles. Finn swallowed. "You can go on to lunch, Darby. And take two pickles for yourself and your sister. I know how much you both like them."

Darby nearly dropped his pencil. "Really? You'd let me take two pickles? And grant me leave to go to lunch early, too?" As soon as the words left his mouth, Darby looked at the ceiling and back and tightened his lips as though uttering the words would void the privilege.

Finn's heart warmed in spite of himself. The favor to his faithful—albeit slow-paced—shop boy must have meant more to Darby than a new pony to a child. "Aye. But mind you, I can't extend such a gift every day."

"Oh, that I know, sir. Thank ye. And ye can be sure I'll be back on time from lunch."

Finn chuckled as Darby handed him the account, then scurried to lunch, clutching two fine pickles he wrapped himself with the care one would usually reserve for diamonds.

Darby kept his promise of a prompt return after lunch. Finn's lightheartedness upon doing a good turn made the afternoon go by more swiftly, despite his disappointment that Colleen didn't appear. Only his regular customers obliged him with a stop by the store. Not that he wasn't grateful; he was. But only Colleen could mend the rip in his heart.

He noticed Joey entering. "Top o' the evening to you," Finn called with forced cheerfulness. "Be right with you, Joey."

He tipped his stylish hat. "Take your time."

Finn completed Mrs. Callahan's order, after which Joey brought several expensive items to the counter.

"You're buying quite a few things today, Joey. Expecting a big Christmas, I see." Joey's bill would keep Finn living in style for a month.

"I have many gifts to give. I must not let anyone go without during the season of our Savior's birth."

"Those on your list will be happy indeed." Finn inspected Joey's selections. He placed a forefinger on a diamond-shaped silver trinket box. "I can't help but wonder if this is for Mary McGuire. She's been eyeing this box and the heart-shaped one for a while now, but I know she can't afford either on her own. You wouldn't be having eyes for her now, would you?"

"No indeed. I don't even know who she is, if you want to know the plain truth."

Joey's evasive answer left Finn more puzzled than ever. How could such a wealthy and attractive man as Joey not appear to know anyone in town, nor be known by anyone? Usually a rich man had more friends than he could count. He remembered the old Irish proverb: "Sweet is the voice of the man who has wealth." Surely Joey's voice was sweet to people other than Finn.

He tried again. "I'm sure some pretty lassie around here has caught your eye."

Joey chuckled. "I'm afraid not. No, 'tis a bachelor's life for me."

"Not if the women around here have anything to say about that, I'd venture."

The men enjoyed a hearty laugh before Joey brought up another topic. "I heard Miss Sullivan had a bit of trouble with some stray sheep last night. Is that so?"

" 'Tis so." Surprised, Finn leaned toward Joey. "Where did you hear such a thing?"

"Fences have ears."

"If only they had mouths as well, then they could have reminded Ross to fix the gap." Finn let out a breath. "I didn't know you were acquainted with Miss Sullivan." He observed once again Joey's magnificently tailored attire and otherwise impeccable appearance, along with his poise. The idea that he knew Colleen caused jealousy to visit.

"I have never spoken to her. I only know of her and her máthair. And Ross."

Finn took in a breath with such exertion that a whistle escaped his lips. "You know Ross?"

"I know about Ross. He is one who needs mercy and grace more than the average man."

Finn snorted. "If he did a lick of work, I would have sympathy for him, and showing mercy would be easy."

"Agreed." Joey's tone carried such weight that, feeling chastised, Finn shifted from one foot to the other. "I know Miss Sullivan needs more help. Managing the farm has gotten to be too much for Ross."

"Ross and the bottle, that is," Finn muttered.

"Never mind that. I know someone who can help."

"You do?"

"Yes. You are familiar with the Wild Boar and Grey Goat Inn?"

Finn nodded.

"Go there now and ask for Patrick. He's an excellent overseer, and I happen to know that he's in need of work. He was just let go from his old job."

Finn wasn't sure exactly which Patrick Joey meant, but there was no arguing with the man. No sooner had he issued his edict than he turned on his heel and disappeared.

Feeling compelled to obey, Finn grabbed his coat,

asked Darby to keep a close eye on the store, and rushed four blocks to the inn. When he entered, several men he recognized waved their greetings. Normally Finn would have stopped to talk, but he knew his mission was too important for him to allow himself the luxury of exchanging pleasantries. He had to find Patrick.

He looked and could identify almost every man present. He had known most since childhood. Others he recognized from church. Almost every man patronized his store at one time or another. Yet—unusual for such a gathering in Dublin—none of them went by the name of the beloved saint who'd brought Christianity to Ireland.

"What can I get fer ye?" asked the burly, unshaven innkeeper.

"Nothing to drink, thank you, Bryan, but you may be able to help me. I seek a man by the name of Patrick."

Bryan shifted his glance from one side of the room to the other. "Patrick? I know a lot of Patricks."

"I'm looking for the Patrick who's an overseer."

"Oh, that Patrick. Why do you want to meet with him? Would he be owin' ye money?"

"No." Finn was glad he wasn't on a mission to collect a debt since Bryan protected his patrons. "I understand he's looking for work. He was just let go at his old job, if my source tells me right."

"So ye're lookin' to hire him at the store?" Bryan narrowed his eyes. "I don't know if that would work out so good. He's used to the outdoors, not bein' inside all day."

"Shouldn't you let him speak for himself?" Finn snapped, then thought better of it. "Anyhow, it doesn't matter. I'm not looking for help at the store. A friend of mine who owns a farm needs a new man, and Patrick was recommended to me by one of my best customers."

"Oh." Bryan cocked his head and looked at Finn squarely. "That changes things. I'll see if he wants to talk to ye." For the first time since he'd offered Finn a drink, Bryan grinned.

Finn waited until the innkeeper emerged from the back with a strapping young man with a full head of straight red hair and muscles evident beneath his shirt. Even before introductions were made, Finn recognized Patrick Dempsey as an employee of the successful Douglas farm.

"I understand you are looking for farmwork?" Finn ventured.

"Sure I am. The sooner the better, I say. The wife is

gettin' low on food for us, and our brood's not wantin' to live on love," Patrick answered in a brogue as thick as clotted cream.

"Weren't you working on the Douglas farm?" Finn sought to confirm.

"Aye, but not anymore. The old man let me go. Seems he had a nephew he liked better. I'd like to see him do my job half as well." Spitting the words, Patrick squinted his eyes and peered at a group of men gambling on a game of cards.

"I hope you can live up to such a bold statement." Though Finn's words offered a challenge, he could discern from the man's muscles that he knew how to work a hoe.

"Aye, I can, and I do. I can fell a tree faster than a beaver and coax more milk and offspring out of the livestock than most of the other farmhands in the parish."

"That's good to hear."

"So who's lookin'? Certainly not you."

"No. But Miss Colleen Sullivan's overseer could use a hand."

"You mean Ross O'Hara?"

"Aye."

"I don't know. I understand he loves the bottle more

than he does his work. Or maybe I shouldn't be confidin' such a thing."

" 'Tis no confidence. Everyone knows Ross doesn't do his job. That's why they could use some help out there. Ross is pretty easygoing. He shouldn't give you much trouble. Not if you do an honest day's work. And from the looks of you, I think you do."

"Aye. I've worked with drunkards before. I can do it again. Ye want me to go an' see her about the job tomorrow mornin'?"

Though Joey had insisted that Finn take on this errand, suddenly he realized that he had no right to tend to the affairs of the Sullivan farm, especially without mentioning his intentions to Colleen first. "Uh, you might better let me put in a good word for you."

"I'd be obliged. Can I buy ye a drink in return fer the favor?"

"No, thank you. I must return to my store."

Finn's stomach churned as he left the inn. He had followed Joey's advice without question, feeling compelled. In his heart, he knew Joey would never mislead him, yet now he had regrets. Would Colleen be upset with him for interfering? Debating was useless now; he had made a promise to Patrick, and he had to keep it. He would just have to face the music, that's all.

Later, after he closed the store, Finn didn't delay in going to the Sullivan farm. *Lord, please let her be grateful, not angry.*

Busy discussing the week's menu with Cook and granting her permission to take home leftovers from lunch to her family, Colleen didn't realize she had a visitor until the maid announced Finn's arrival. Her heart started to beat in a noticeable way. All day she'd been fighting the urge to go to Finn's store and apologize to him for being cold when he chastised her about Ross. Much of what Finn had said about Ross was right. Yet she had to show Finn that he needed to see her side of the story—even if that meant not seeing him in spite of her yearning.

Not expecting guests, Colleen hadn't taken time to look her best. She wished to freshen her appearance, but making Finn wait too long would be rude. Colleen instructed the maid to fetch a cup of tea for Finn and make him comfortable in the parlor. That would buy her enough time to give Cook final menu approval for the next day and to smooth her hair.

Moments later, when she saw him sitting straight in a velvet chair, enjoying the tea, she stopped her pace for an instant. She could imagine greeting him each evening after a day at the shop, asking about his customers and about the popular patterns and fabrics from abroad. She dreamed about pleasing him with his favorite dishes and sharing time by the fire each evening. But such fantasies were just that—only fantasies.

He arose when she entered. "Good evening, Colleen."

"Good evening." She sat in her favorite chair across from him.

"I ask your forgiveness for appearing unannounced. My news is important."

"Of course." She knew if she expected compassion from him, she had to demonstrate it in kind. "You are welcome here anytime."

His countenance brightened. "So you forgive me for the unkind words I had for Ross last evening?"

"Your words were said in a state of vexation." She cast her gaze upon the floor. "They held a grain of truth, I'm sorry to say."

"I want what's best for you, though I'm sorry if I appeared to be harsh."

"You mean well," she said in all truthfulness. "So tell me, what is your news?"

"No need for me to delay in telling you. I—I asked Patrick Dempsey about working here. He'd like to take you up on the offer, if you'll have him."

She didn't know whether to feel grateful or vexed by his interference. "You did what?"

"I spoke to Patrick about working with Ross. I wouldn't have known he was available, either, except that Joey told me." He tapped the bottom of his mug a few times on the arm of the chair.

"Joey? You mean that customer of yours who comes in and buys enough goods to keep a brood of twenty and a staff of servants fed and clothed in fine style?"

"That's the one."

She shook her head. "He certainly is a mysterious one. No one seems to know anything about him."

"Maybe not, but he seems to know everything about everyone else. Patrick is a mighty good overseer. I'd hire him myself if I owned a farm. And just think—you'd be doing a good deed. He has a wife and children, and he needs the job."

Colleen thought for a moment. "I suppose I can afford to pay another man, especially if he'll do a good job."

"I think he will."

She decided to be pleased with Finn rather than vexed. After all, he had taken a risk to do her a favor. "Please tell him to report for work tomorrow morning at six."

"I will." Finn paused. "Your trust means much to me."

"Of course I trust you. You are an honorable man."

"I did a good deed myself today for Darby. A small thing, really. But it made him so happy that I felt happy, too."

She wondered what he meant, but details weren't forthcoming. But did the deed itself matter? Only Finn's compassion did. The idea that he had changed his ways toward his shop boy warmed her heart. "Aye, you are seeing that the rewards of Christian charity flow both ways."

"Indeed they do."

A spontaneous thought occurred to her. "Oh, I do have a question for you."

"Aye?"

Though a sudden feeling of shyness visited, she didn't let it stop her from posing her query. "Would you be so kind as to accept our invitation to Christmas Eve dinner?"

"Christmas Eve dinner?"

She didn't expect him to seem so taken aback and decided to mitigate his unease with jesting. "Aye. On December twenty-fourth, it is. At least I'm pretty sure that's the date."

"Indeed!" He laughed.

"You won't need to tend the store, since Christmas Eve falls on Sunday this year," she pointed out in a tone that reminded him of a dangling carrot in front of a horse's nose.

"But it's back to work for me on Christmas Day."

Why did he stall? Bowing to etiquette, she offered him an escape. "Your hesitation suggests you have other plans. I understand."

"No!" he rushed to assure her. "I have no plans at all."

"Are you sure?"

"Yes, I'm sure."

"Good." Her expression revealed more relief than she intended. "I hope your máthair will join us as well."

"I would be delighted to accept your invitation, and I feel confident in saying that my máthair will consent."

After the door shut behind him, she could hear him whistle a cheery tune. Happiness had made itself abundant among the Sullivans and Donohues.

Chapter 6

Mrs. Sullivan entered the house, back from posting letters in town. She didn't bother to give her usual account of the people she saw there, but came straight to the point. "I passed Finn Donohue turning out of our lane. He must have come by for a visit?"

"Yes, Máthair. You needn't worry. All was right and proper. I did invite him in to sit by the fire and partake of tea. He was the perfect gentleman. The servants will attest to that."

"Aye," Cook said.

"I find no call for such dramatics. You are a lady, and he is a gentleman," Mrs. Sullivan confirmed.

"I know." Trust between Colleen and her máthair had never been in question, so she pitied Finn for his admission of pain suffered at the hands of his fáthair's negligence. She mused about how blessed she was to have such a devoted parent. She could only hope that she could imitate her máthair successfully once she married and, if it pleased the Lord, that He would bless her with children.

Colleen addressed Cook. "Mrs. Sullivan and I shall depart to the dining room. Please see that dinner is served."

"Aye, Miss Sullivan."

As soon as she and her máthair were seated at the modest table, Colleen filled her in on the rest of the conversation. "I did invite Finn and his máthair to Christmas Eve dinner. I knew you wouldn't mind."

"Not at all. We are blessed, and I am grateful for any opportunity to share our blessings with others." Mrs. Sullivan gave her a sly look. "But surely our local merchant didn't come by to get himself invited to dinner."

"No. He wanted to tell me about a new farmhand who can help us around here. Patrick Dempsey. He was let go from the Douglas farm and is looking for a new position." She regretted the need to express her next sentiment. "After the incident with the sheep, I think it's time we hired someone else."

"With reluctance, I agree." She sighed. "So you're going to do just as Finn says? You're going to hire this man Patrick?"

"With your permission."

"Aye, I give my permission. We've been in need of a reliable overseer around here for a long time. I just didn't have the courage to tell Ross."

"We don't have to let Ross go. We'll let Patrick help him, that's all."

"Because Finn Donohue told you so."

"Aye." The idea that a man cared enough about her to make such a suggestion didn't offend Colleen, even though she considered herself an independent. Instead, she felt strangely safe. She liked that feeling. She liked it very much.

Colleen didn't relish her next task, but she needed to let Ross know what was happening before Patrick's arrival the following day. She sent a messenger to the farm-hands' quarters and summoned Ross to her study. He wasn't long in appearing. To Colleen's surprise, he had combed his hair and wore a fresh change of clothes.

"I know what ye're goin' to say before ye even say it," he said without accepting the seat she offered. "Ye're goin' to let me go. Well, I s'pose I deserve it. Ye've been kind to me long enough."

Ross, whom Colleen's máthair had told her was once a proud man, appeared beaten. Colleen could look into his face and see that he had once been comely, but drink, to which he took in sorrow after losing his wife and young child to illness, had taken the joy from his being. He looked at his shoes and slumped his shoulders.

"We're not firing you," Colleen said.

"Why not?" He looked up, defiance in his eyes. "I deserve it, just like your man Finn Donohue said."

"Don't you remember the apostle Paul's letter to Titus? 'Not by works of righteousness which we have done, but according to his mercy he saved us.'"

"So?"

"So how could we turn you out when the Lord has been so merciful to us? I only ask that you accept the help that we are offering you."

"Help?" Suspicion colored his voice.

"Aye. We have employed Patrick Dempsey to take

over the main duties, but we want you to stay on and show him the ropes."

He narrowed his eyes. "And then what?"

"It will be as it always has been," Colleen assured him. "You may stay as long as you like."

"Are ye sure?"

"I am."

Ross fiddled with the brim of the hat he held in his hand. Staring at it, he nodded. "Thank ye." Though his voice was barely audible, Colleen knew he meant his expression of gratitude as surely as if he had shouted it from the rooftops. "I—I'll try to do better by ye."

"I know. And I'll pray for you," she promised.

"I wish ye would. God prefers prayers to tears."

On Christmas Eve, the Donohue carriage rolled down the rutted lane of the Sullivan farm, toward their white-washed house that appeared both large and inviting. Mrs. Donohue lurched to one side, almost bumping her head.

"Seems to me any family with as much wealth as the Sullivans could do a better job o' keepin' up their road," she remarked in her lilting Irish brogue. "I don't know if we should have come 'ere for dinner tonight. I don't expect to suffer bodily harm all in the name o' dinner, even if 'tis Christmas Eve."

"You'll recover, sure as I'm sitting here." Finn's voice remained gentle.

She righted the basket she held in her lap. "I just hope my pie survives the trip."

"No amount of bumping will affect its taste," he assured her.

Finn knew why his máthair seemed out of sorts. Reclusive except for trudging to and from work since his fáthair abandoned them, she wasn't accustomed to sharing any meal, even a holiday dinner, with others. Finn had taken a risk in agreeing to the dinner on behalf of his máthair.

As he predicted, she had acted withdrawn and irritable ever since he told her about their plans. He half expected her to feign illness that night. To his surprise, she had instructed her maid to style her thinning gray hair in a flattering manner. For the first time, she wore the new bonnet Finn had ordered from the same milliner Colleen employed. He noted she seemed uncomfortable in her redingote, tugging now and again on the fur-trimmed sleeves that no doubt seemed bulky and unnatural to her. As the maid helped her with the redingote, he had been pleased to see she had even chosen to wear her new blue winter pelisse.

Employing her own maid and wearing stylish attire were two aspects of her new life that Mrs. Donohue had not adjusted to readily; serving came to her more easily than being served. But she had earned what little bit of luxury he could now afford her, and Finn planned for his máthair to become even more accustomed to living well as the store grew more and more prosperous. According to his ledgers, prosperity wouldn't wane soon.

Looking over at his máthair, he wondered if she secretly was glad he had suggested they have dinner with the Sullivans and was only experiencing nervousness and regret now that the time had arrived. Finn sent up a silent prayer that she would relax.

He decided to help by distracting her. He pointed to the house. "Look. There's a candle lit in the window."

"So 'tis." She nodded. "Pretty. Colleen is the youngest in the family; am I right?

"Right you are, Máthair. It's just her and her máthair. No doubt Miss Colleen is the one who lit the candle, being the youngest family member. They are very traditional folks, you know. I can tell by the wares Miss Colleen buys at the store and the tales she tells me."

Mrs. Donohue harrumphed and looked out the window. "The tradition seems more comely in a house where there is a child."

Finn didn't answer. Instead, he thought about Colleen's innocent ways. Her angelic face gave her the aura of a beautiful child, but she was so much more. He couldn't resist thinking about being married to Colleen. Thoughts of her had only increased since she agreed to hire Patrick without any reticence. The fact of her trust told him that her heart was growing softer toward him. She would make a good wife.

At the same time, his increased compassion toward others was being rewarded even though prizes were not what he sought. Since he had grown kinder toward Darby, the youth had been quick about his chores, and the store looked cleaner and tidier as a result. Finn had also resolved to be more patient with those in arrears with their payments to him, praying that he would strike the right balance of mercy and justice. Surely Colleen would have been proud of his progress had she been able to look over his shoulder, but he had a feeling he didn't need to boast. No doubt his demeanor revealed his new way of thinking.

Colleen. His thoughts never had trouble returning to her. If they wed, one day she would bear him beautiful children. Their first girl would be named Mary. She would light their Christmas Eve candle. The candle acted as a symbol of welcome to the Virgin and Joseph as they traveled looking for shelter, just as they had done on the night of the Savior's birth.

"Ye're quiet. Deep in thought, eh?" Mrs. Donohue interrupted his musings. "Ye are quite fond o' Miss Sullivan, ain't ye?"

No point in not telling the truth. "Aye."

"Ye think she'd consent to be your wife?"

The thought, one he had dwelt on for so long, sounded so permanent falling from his máthair's lips. He gulped. "Would that please you?"

"Aye. She'd be lucky to have ye."

"I think she can make me happy. Very happy."

She chuckled. "Ye know what they say. Marriages are all happy. It's havin' breakfast together that causes all the trouble."

He laughed. "I can imagine having breakfast with her with no trouble at all." He cut his glance to her and noticed a slight smile on his máthair's lips. Her approval meant so much. With her blessing, he knew pursuing Colleen was right.

The carriage stopped.

Mrs. Donohue clutched the basket that contained the dessert she had prepared and stared at it. Finn noticed that her eyes appeared to be blank.

"What's wrong, Máthair?"

"I'm not feelin' so well, Finn. I think I'd like to go home." Her smile had vanished.

He knew that her fears, not illness, spurred this new protest. "You'll be thinking nothing of the kind. You'll dine with the Sullivans and enjoy every minute. 'Tis not as though you'll be among strangers. You know Mrs. Sullivan from church."

"Aye, I suppose she's pleasant enough." She kept her gaze on the pie.

With a gentle motion, Finn took the basket from his máthair and then helped her disembark from the carriage. She stepped slowly toward the house, as though she faced execution rather than a pleasant meal. In moments they had arrived at the door and were greeted by Colleen and Mrs. Sullivan.

No matter how many times he saw Colleen, Finn

had to control himself to keep from sighing in admiration. This night she looked especially lovely. Though dressed in the most superb of her finery—a picture of perfection in red and green—she could have been wearing the milkmaid's rags and still presented the image of beauty. Her eyes shone and sparkled just like the stars. Burning candles offered a flattering light to her form, catching the sparkle of her hair and pearl-like teeth. When she greeted him with a hello, the world melted.

"I brought a mincemeat pie," Mrs. Donohue informed Colleen, bringing him back to practical matters. Mrs. Donohue's voice sounded tentative, as though she wondered if her offering would be accepted.

"Splendid! It will be a wonderful accompaniment to our Christmas pudding." Colleen sent them both a gracious smile.

Finn watched his máthair's reaction. As he expected, Colleen's pleased expression caused her posture to relax. Even better, if Colleen noticed that Mrs. Donohue felt uncomfortable, she didn't let on in her countenance or conversation. Mrs. Sullivan was just as welcoming.

Relieved, Finn was determined to keep all the women, especially Colleen, smiling during the entire visit. He tried all night to be witty, and Colleen's repeated laughter and smiles rewarded him, convincing him of his success. When Colleen asked him if he would offer grace before the meal, Finn felt grateful that he had used his foresight to memorize a few words of gratitude. Yet his planned speech didn't materialize. Instead, the blessing he offered came from his heart and, to his ears, sounded lovelier than anything he could have written on his own.

Afterward, Finn stuffed himself on spiced beef and a variety of accompaniments and partook of both the mincemeat pie and Christmas pudding. After dinner, he patted his belly and inwardly congratulated himself on the way, in spite of the setback he'd suffered as a child, his prosperity allowed him to enjoy such fine company and food.

After the meal, Colleen again set the table and placed on it a loaf of bread made with caraway seeds and raisins, a pitcher of milk, and a candle of beeswax that was large enough to offer light for several hours. The back door was left unlocked so that Mary and Joseph, or any wandering traveler, could partake of the dinner.

"The two o' ye have set out a fine meal, ye have," Mrs. Donohue commented. "Mary and Joseph would be proud to eat here if they passed by."

Finn sent his máthair a smile, noting that her evening was progressing as well as the greeting had promised. Despite her initial anxiety, she had taken well to Colleen and Mrs. Sullivan. Soon the older women chatted like old friends. Earlier that evening, Mrs. Sullivan had even suggested that Mrs. Donohue join the church sewing circle. To his delight, Finn's máthair accepted with little hesitation. Surely the Lord had a hand in getting his reluctant máthair to become involved with new friends.

He said a silent prayer, thanking the Lord that his máthair, who had spent her youth as a servant, was accepted by the Sullivans without reservation. Then again, Colleen and her máthair were known for their free expressions of Christian charity.

Finn returned his thoughts to the present. "I hope someone stops by to eat such a fine meal." He admired the table. "Perhaps a traveler on his way out of town."

"Do you really hope someone stops?" Colleen asked. "I didn't think you cared enough about people you think of as ne'er-do-wells to wish they would partake of a free meal."

"Colleen!" Mrs. Sullivan chastised. "What are you thinking, insulting our guest in such a way?"

"I'm sorry, Máthair. And I'm sorry, Finn." Genuine regret colored her face and voice.

"No matter, Colleen. I deserved that remark, and more. I never have had much patience with laziness." He glanced at his máthair. She knew why Finn felt the way he did about irresponsible men.

"Don't let past pains affect the present," Mrs. Donohue said. " 'Tis time to let all that go." She reached over and patted his shoulder.

Finn wasn't so sure. He changed the subject. "Has anyone ever stopped by in past years?"

"No, sadly." Colleen shrugged. "I don't expect any-one to stop by tonight, either. But we put the food out, all the same. And we hope. And we pray."

Chapter 7

As the evening waned, Finn wished he could think of a reason to prolong the festivities. The four of them had just about run out of conversation, but he was comfortable by the fire in the parlor, and he didn't want to leave Colleen's presence.

Finn was ready to express regret that the evening needed to come to a close, when they heard a knock on the door.

"Who might that be?" he asked.

"I think I know. Excuse me." Colleen rose from her chair and disappeared. A few moments later, she reappeared with a young girl who looked to be on the cusp of womanhood.

Finn studied the girl. Her eyes were a stunning shade of blue, and her hair an appealing shade of red. He recalled an old proverb: "If you meet a red-haired woman, you'll meet a crowd." No doubt the boys in Dublin fought over her, even though beside Colleen, not even the girl's brilliant hair could put her above the beauty of the one Finn loved. Only after he had made that silent observation did he realize that the girl's clothing, though clean, showed signs of repeated mending and her shoes were well worn.

"This is Mary O'Connell," Colleen explained.

"Oh. Mary." Finn realized what was happening. Mary had been engaged to extinguish the Christmas Eve candle. According to tradition, only a girl bearing her name could extinguish it. No doubt Mary had several other houses to visit that evening. Though her name enjoyed popularity in Ireland, not every house was blessed with a little girl by that name.

The family followed Mary to the window. She extinguished the candle with a delicate breath. After the light ceased, everyone present stood in awed silence. Finn observed the deep night, lit by twinkling stars, its silence broken by the occasional bleating of a sheep and braying of a goat. The animals reminded Finn of the way angels announced the Savior's birth to shepherds watching their flocks. How magnificent and startling their glory must have appeared amid an otherwise silent night.

After a moment, Colleen's sweet voice broke the silence. "Thank you, Mary."

The girl nodded. " 'Tis beautiful, isn't it?"

"Aye," Mrs. Sullivan agreed.

Colleen handed the girl a sack that Finn had watched Colleen prepare earlier. Mary's family would enjoy the several slices of meat, potatoes, and two slices each of pie and cake. Colleen also handed the girl a few coins. Finn thought Colleen paid too well for the small task Mary performed but realized that Colleen's generosity was essential to her nature and part of the occasion.

Mary's eyes lit with gratitude. She curtsied. "Aye, mistress. Thank ye."

"Thank you," Finn added.

Mary's glance caught his gaze, and in the look he discerned desperation. Perhaps the food Colleen provided would be the only Christmas feast Mary's family would know that year. Without warning, his heart moved toward the girl, and he reached for money in his pocket. Surely his máthair and he could do without a few extra coins. He surrendered a few pence, and her open mouth and her eyes lit with thankfulness were a far greater reward than he felt he deserved. Suddenly he wished he could do more.

"Oh, thank you, sir!" Mary curtsied to him.

Soon the girl disappeared into the frigid night. Finn wondered what type of home she might be going to at evening's end. He said a silent prayer for Mary, her family, and the world's disadvantaged. He remembered the Savior reminding His disciples that the poor would always be with the world. Truly Finn could not help everyone, but he could touch the few people the Lord might see fit to place in his path. He prayed for future discernment.

A thump sounded just as he finished his impromptu prayer.

"What was that?" Colleen turned her head in the direction of the noise.

"I don't know," Mrs. Sullivan answered. "It sounds as though it came from the dining room."

"Surely no traveler is visiting us, after all these years of having no one stop by on Christmas Eve," Colleen wondered aloud. She took Finn by the forearm and looked into his eyes. "Oh, I am glad you are here."

Finn felt his courage emerge, thanks to her touch

and the dependence on him that her look demonstrated. "I'm sure whoever our visitor is means us no harm. Indeed, he could be a wandering traveler who is aware of our tradition of offering a meal. Or perhaps it's simply the cat knocking over a bowl."

"Perhaps," Colleen agreed. She relaxed. "I suppose it's not even worth investigating."

They resumed conversation until a sound that seemed to be the foot of a chair dragging across the wood floors drew attention. Finn sensed the others in the room stiffen. With a tone that conveyed more confidence than he experienced at that moment, Finn said, "I'll see who— or what—it is. Ladies, please stay here. I would not wish harm to come to you, should our visitor be a thief."

"Be careful, Finn," Colleen begged.

Her words fortified him enough that he could smile. "I will."

Finn felt a touch of fear but managed to tiptoe into the hallway leading to the dining room.

Lord, I petition Thee for protection.

Once he reached the threshold, he peered into the room.

What is this?

Curiosity and fascination left him immobile. A man,

dressed in a coat that had more holes than cloth and a shirt missing the two top buttons, had accepted their unspoken invitation and sat at the table. At that moment, he ate bread. The way he tore at the food, ripping it with his teeth, reminded Finn of a hungry dog. After the man had finished the slice of bread, he picked up the pitcher of milk and poured a goblet full, ignoring spill-age on the table. He then gulped down the liquid so quickly, Finn wondered if he even tasted the milk.

Napkins were provided, but the man paid them no heed. Instead, between every few bites he wiped his mouth on his sleeve. Finn wondered if he could even find a clean spot amid such dirt. He contemplated offering the ragged man a suit of his own clothes but decided against it when he saw that the other man's frame, though thin, was larger than his own. A beggar would give little thought to precise tailoring, but this man wouldn't be able to squeeze into any of Finn's gar-ments. Perhaps he would offer to let the man come into the store for a new suit of clothing on Monday.

The thought startled him. Would such a thought have occurred to his mind only days ago? He realized that his heart had changed. The change felt good.

Reluctant to disturb the man since he obviously

hadn't eaten for some time, Finn watched him devour the remaining milk and bread.

"Is everything all right, Finn?" Colleen called from the next room.

"Aye. Please don't worry. All is taken care of." He expected the man to look up, but he kept eating.

"Is there anything we can do?" Colleen asked.

"Stay where you are." Realizing the beggar must have heard their exchange, Finn knew the time had come for him to speak with the man.

When Finn entered the room and approached the table, the man set down the goblet with a thud. "Afraid of me, eh, Finn?"

The voice sounded familiar, and the man knew his name. But he didn't know any beggars. At least, in the past he'd never looked when he passed them on the street, and he'd blocked his ears from hearing their cries for spare farthings. He decided that his indifference to the plight of others would change.

He screwed up his courage. "I'm not afraid. I—I thought I might offer you a suit of clothes, or a blanket from my store if you need one."

"Ye did, did ye?" Even through the dirt caked on his face, Finn could see that the man was both pleased and surprised. "Well, ye seem to 'ave made some progress in your attitude toward those less fortunate than yourself."

"Less fortunate? Fortune has nothing to do with my success. I work hard for everything I get and put my faith in the good Lord that He will see fit to reward my puny efforts." Despite his sympathy for the pathetic soul, Finn's anger grew. "I'm not a rich man's son. Any success I have, I owe to my máthair's hard work—demeaning work she had to take on to support us and lift us out of poverty. I'm not about to throw away my money. I have finally reached the point of prosperity where I can provide my máthair a more leisurely life, a life she deserves. I see no reason to waste my hard-earned money on people who are too lazy to work."

"Too lazy to work, eh? Is that what you think about me?"

Suddenly Finn felt nervous. Something seemed strangely familiar about this man, and Finn's confidence in his answers was starting to wane. "I—I don't know about you."

"You don't? Are you sure?" The man stared into his face.

Finn gasped. Those eyes! He had seen the same eyes just yesterday. No. It couldn't be. It couldn't be! "Joey?"

He nodded. " 'Tis I."

"But—but what happened to you?" Finn couldn't help but stare at the man's attire. "Where is your fine hat, your beautiful suit? Why are you dressed in rags not fit for a dog's bed?"

Joey shrugged. "Like the apostle Paul, I can live with much or with little, whatever is the Lord's provision. I have found that people respond to me more favorably when I pose as a rich man than when I appear like this." He looked down at his clothes and chuckled, but Finn heard no rancor.

"But only yesterday, you bought many fine Christmas gifts. And you paid in gold."

"Aye, and those gifts will be loved by the little children who have nothing else."

"Little children?"

"Aye, and their parents, too." Joey looked into Finn's eyes. "So what do you think of me now that I'm not dressed in finery? Now that I have not a pence to me name?"

"Did you lose your fortune so quickly?"

"Aye, I did, and I don't miss it," Joey confessed. "So now that I am poor and can no longer patronize your store, has your opinion of me changed?"

"What can I say? Can't you see I'm too flabbergasted to speak?"

"So the Blarney stone vanished, did it?" He chuckled in a kind way. "I know, lad. This must come as quite a shock. But ye must learn from seeing me here tonight that not every less fortunate person is a ne'er-do-well like your fáthair."

"How—how do you know about my fáthair?"

"Your resentment about him has eaten at ye like a tapeworm. Ye've let his actions affect your outlook on life, and because of that, ye've thrown away much happiness and peace that could have been yours, had ye been more trustin'. The time has come to forgive your fáthair and to enjoy the abundant life that can be yours. Can ye not see that now?"

"There must be something you're not telling me. What is it? What do you know about my fáthair?"

Joey shook his head.

"You mean you don't have some sort of story to tell me that will make things right, some facts I didn't know that will prove me wrong about his character? Some evidence that shows I should forgive him?"

"That would make ye happy, wouldn't it? To think that your fáthair had some good reason for leavin', other than to follow the leprechauns? If he did, that reason 'asn't been revealed to me. Nay, I'm sorry, but ye must be stronger than that. Without any explanation or increased understanding, I'm askin' ye to forgive him and let go of the past. If ye don't, ye'll never find the true happiness God has planned for your life."

Finn hesitated. "What you're asking isn't easy."

"I know. Ye've been carrying around a lot of bitterness for years. Too many years. If ye're not cautious, that bitterness will keep on eatin' at ye 'til ye're an old man, gnarled with anger and alone in the world."

Finn swallowed.

"Ye don't want that for yourself, do ye?"

"Nay." His voice was but a whisper.

"I leave you with Psalm 145:8: 'The Lord is gracious, and full of compassion; slow to anger, and of great mercy.'"

Finn nodded. "I understand."

"I'm glad to hear it."

"I'll never see you again, will I?"

"Whether or not you see me again is not for me to decide."

Chapter 8

What do you think is going on in there?" Mrs. Sullivan whispered. "He's been in there a long time."

Colleen didn't want to give her máthair reason to fret, but she was concerned, as well. What if Finn faced trouble? Her heart beat faster with the thought. Like it or not, she couldn't control the fact that her world would be turned upside down if anything happened to Finn.

"Why don't I go take a look?" she suggested in a whisper.

Mrs. Sullivan hesitated. "I don't know."

Mrs. Donohue intervened. "Please?"

Colleen nodded then tiptoed into the doorway of the dining room. When she saw the scene, she froze. Finn conversed with a man in rags, a man whose relaxed posture showed he was no threat to anyone. Yet his face looked familiar. She squinted. Could it be?

Joey!

Though she hadn't spoken aloud, Finn turned to her, obviously sensing her presence.

"Colleen."

"Finn, what is the meaning of this?"

Finn turned to face her and looked into her eyes. As soon as he did, she could see that something in him—to his very soul—had changed. "It seems I learned a lesson today."

"A lesson? How? Why is Joey dressed in such tattered clothing? Why did he stop at our house to eat humble food, when surely he must have a fine Christmas meal to go to anywhere he likes in Dublin? I don't understand."

"I don't understand everything, either. Perhaps Joey will enlighten us."

Following the turn of Finn's head, Colleen peered in the direction of the dining room table. Joey had vanished.

A look of puzzlement and alarm colored Finn's expression. "Joey! Where are you?"

Colleen watched as Finn strode through the kitchen and flew out the back door. She could hear him calling Joey's name, his voice carrying over the fields. Colleen didn't move. She sensed that Joey didn't want to be found, and wouldn't be.

Mrs. Sullivan approached from behind and touched Colleen on the shoulder. "Whatever is the matter? Who is Finn looking for?"

"Joey. He was here, and then he just disappeared." Colleen snapped her fingers. "Like that."

"Joey?" Mrs. Donohue parroted. "The same Joey who patronizes the store?"

"Aye," Colleen responded.

Mrs. Sullivan's eyes widened. "Why, I never heard of such a thing. Where are our manners? He's been so good to Finn, we must invite him to partake of some of our food. There's plenty left."

"No, Máthair, he has already partaken." Colleen pointed to what little remained of the bread and milk.

"He ate the meal we set out?"

"He certainly did," Colleen affirmed.

Mouth hanging open, Mrs. Donohue put her hand to her chest. "Are you meaning to say that Joey is actually a beggar?"

"I don't know," Colleen admitted. "All I know is what I saw, and the change I see now in Finn's face."

Finn approached, bringing the outside frost with him. "Did you find Joey?"

"No. He melted into the night. He has always had that habit. Except this time, I don't think we'll ever see him again."

" 'Tisn't so!" Mrs. Donohue protested. "Why, he was one of our best customers, he was."

"Yes, Máthair," Finn agreed. "But my business is thriving, and while I'll miss seeing Joey, I now have many wealthy patrons. But I know he came here to teach me a lesson about life, not to fill my coffers. From now on, I'll make an honest profit from the store, as I always have, but there will be a change. I won't be stingy any longer. I'll be generous with my time and money."

"So that's what he came to teach ye, eh? To throw away your money?".

"I won't throw it away, Máthair. There will be plenty for us, but I will use more of what I have to God's glory, not simply hoard it."

Mrs. Donohue smiled. "That's a right good thing, 'tis."

"And there's something else. I tell each of you here

tonight, I'll never again look down upon anyone less fortunate. First, Colleen took me to see the orphans, and even though they didn't have a mind to, they worked on my cold heart. And now, seeing Joey as he was caused me to realize all the more that it is not a person's wealth that matters, but what is in his heart."

"But your fáthair. Can ye forgive 'im?" Mrs. Donohue asked.

Finn's face softened. "I know you forgave him long ago, Máthair. 'Tis high time I did the same. So yes, I forgive him. And from now on, I will pray every day for him, wherever he might be."

Colleen felt as though a long-standing burden had been lifted from her back. When Finn reached for her hand, she allowed him to take it.

"I think 'tis high time you and I share in a cup of tea, don't you, Mrs. Donohue?" Mrs. Sullivan asked.

Mrs. Donohue studied Finn and Colleen, a tickle of light entering her eyes. "Aye."

As the older women departed into the kitchen, Colleen and Finn took a seat in the parlor.

"Finn, I must say, I cannot believe your change of heart. Surely there is more to this than meets the eye. I can't help but wonder if Joey might indeed be an angel."

"An angel?" He stroked his chin. "I hadn't thought of that. He does have a habit of disappearing without a trace. But I tell you what. It doesn't matter who or what Joey is. What matters is that God used him to teach me a lesson I needed to learn."

"I knew your heart was never so hard as you let on, Finn," Colleen said. "You were hurt, and pain can be an awful thing to overcome on your own."

"True. I suppose I needed help. You, for one. Taking me to the orphanage like that. Those boys touched my heart that day. And they're the first ones I have a mind to help more, Colleen."

"Oh, that would be wonderful. The more you speak, the more convinced I am that Joey is an angel."

"It matters not. The only angelic being I care about is sitting beside me."

Colleen felt a blush rise to her cheeks, and she retreated to the shield of formality. "You exaggerate, Mr. Donohue."

"Let me find out. I'd like to court you in earnest, if you'll have me."

Colleen felt her mouth grow dry and her heart beat swiftly. "Court me?"

"Aye. I wasn't worthy before, and I'm really not

worthy now. But all the same, I hope you'll give a humble shopkeeper like me a chance."

"Oh, I'll give you more than a chance."

He took her hands in his. "How your words fill my heart with glee, my beautiful Colleen of Erin. I love you now more than ever. I have always loved you, from the very first time we met."

"And I have always felt the same about you." Her voice came out in a whisper. Suddenly she felt awed by the radiance left by his true repentance. "How I love you, Finn Donohue!"

He took her in his arms and brought his lips closer to hers. Closer, closer, until they made sweet contact. The kiss, so warm and gratifying, was all she dreamed it could have been. The touch expressed and revealed their love for each other better than words ever could.

Epilogue

Finally, the wedding day had arrived, and after a lovely church ceremony, Colleen and Finn were man and wife. Frolicking abounded at the reception, as the popular couple had invited many friends and family to celebrate their special day with them. Patrick, the farmhand Colleen hired, and his family were among the guests. Under his stewardship, the Sullivan farm had become more prosperous than ever.

"Are you ready to give up your bouquet?" Finn asked, looking like royalty in his fine wedding garb. "The girls are waiting."

Colleen regarded the pink and yellow wildflowers in

her bouquet, marveling at the way they complimented the filmy pink and yellow gown she had chosen to wear for the ceremony. More wildflowers were woven throughout her dark hair, standing out brightly amid her shiny locks. She had never felt lovelier, and judging from Finn's expression, she had never appeared to be more beautiful in his eyes.

"I don't blame anyone for wanting such a magnificent souvenir of this day." She let out a happy sigh. "I'm ready." She looked at the throng of young women.

"Toss it to me! Toss it to me!" Colleen heard from several as she tossed her bouquet of spring flowers and shamrocks.

Laughing, she shut her eyes and tossed. The smallest girl, a cousin no more than five years of age, caught the bouquet.

" 'Tis a good thing the superstition of the bouquet is just that—a superstition," Finn joked. "Otherwise, we'd have a lot of spinsters in the family while they waited for her to grow up and marry."

Colleen laughed. Mirth came easily to her that day, and every day since she and Finn had agreed to court, and later to marry. They chose St. Patrick's Day to wed, which proved to be lovely in the spring. Ireland was dressed in her finest greenery. Colleen and Finn liked to think that such a glorious afternoon had been made by the Lord, just for them, to bless their special day.

Pipes and fiddles played in the background, sending out tunes the guests had known since childhood. They feasted on a wedding cake decorated with shamrocks, symbolizing the Father, Son, and Holy Spirit. Even without such traditional symbolism, all who knew the young couple were aware that God was central to their marriage.

Finn took her by the hand. His face radiated exuberance. "I love you, Colleen Donohue."

"Colleen Donohue." Laughter escaped her lips once again. "How many times I said that name to myself, but now it sounds so new and strange—but lovely—coming from your lips."

"Shall I say it until you become accustomed to it?" Finn teased. "Colleen Donohue. Colleen Donohue. Colleen Donohue. Is that enough?"

"It will never be enough."

As Finn drew her close for a kiss, she could only imagine the happiness she would feel being Mrs. Finn Donohue for the rest of her days.

IRISH SODA BREAD

4 to 4½ cups all-purpose flour
1 tsp. salt
3 tsp. baking powder
1 tsp. baking soda
¼ cup sugar
2 cups currants or raisins
¼ cup butter
1 egg
1¾ cup buttermilk

In a large bowl, stir together 4 cups flour and the rest of the dry ingredients. Cut in butter with a pastry blender or two knives until crumbly. In a separate bowl, beat egg slightly and mix with buttermilk. Stir into dry ingredients until blended. Place dough on a floured board and knead 3 minutes or until smooth.

Divide dough in half and shape each half into a smooth, round loaf. Place each loaf in a greased 8-inch cake or pie pan. Press down until dough fills pans. With a sharp, floured knife, cut crosses about ½ inch deep in tops of loaves.

Bake in a 375-degree oven for 35 to 40 minutes or until nicely browned. Makes 2 loaves.

TAMELA HANCOCK MURRAY

Tamela lives in Northern Virginia with her two daughters and her husband of over twenty years. She keeps busy with church and school activities, but in her spare time she's written seven Bible trivia books and twenty Christian romance novels and novellas.

A Letter to Our Readers

Dear Readers:

In order that we might better contribute to your reading enjoyment, we would appreciate your taking a few minutes to respond to the following questions. When completed, please return to the following: Fiction Editor, Barbour Publishing, Inc., P.O. Box 719, Uhrichsville, OH 44683.

1. Did you enjoy reading *Yuletide in Ireland & Wales*?
   ❑ Very much—I would like to see more books like this.
   ❑ Moderately—I would have enjoyed it more if _____

   _____

   _____

2. What influenced your decision to purchase this book?
   (Check those that apply.)
   ❑ Cover   ❑ Back cover copy   ❑ Title   ❑ Price
   ❑ Friends   ❑ Publicity   ❑ Other

3. Which story was your favorite?
   ❑ *Lost and Found*
   ❑ *Colleen of Erin*

4. Please check your age range:
   ❑ Under 18   ❑ 18–24   ❑ 25–34
   ❑ 35–45   ❑ 46–55   ❑ Over 55

5. How many hours per week do you read? _____

Name _____

Occupation _____

Address _____

City _____ State _____ Zip _____

E-mail _____